ROOSTER

By
Edward Pontacoloni

ISBN: 978-1-48356-774-7

This is dedicated to those folks who do what they do with their dogs for the dog's sake . . . for Pete's sake as Tom might say.

Jana, 2008

A STORY'S INVITATION

There is a pooka in this story, a blue butterfly sprite from the once long ago forests of Ireland.

I imagine that this might surprise you. I was surprised, myself. I wasn't sure of it until after our adventure was over, until after old Tom Quinn, the field trialer, had told my wife, Jan. Then Jan told me and, since she was also an eyewitness, she could attest to it firsthand.

If you are not inclined to readily believe in such things as pookas, well then you might go and ask the kids, Mike and Amy. They are pretty familiar with everything that happened, being as they were at the center of it. Well, them and Mike's dog, Rooster. They happen to be away at the Crooked Branch right now, but they should be back shortly. If you want to hang around, I can tell you more while you wait.

Of course, if you're in a hurry to move on, then you might just go and ask Jan's dog, Sparky. He was good friends with the pooka, which is as might be expected, they both being gregarious types. I also think that Sparky possibly is related to pookas in some odd way or another, if not in fact by parentage far back in his ancestry.

To be sure, it is quite possible that all dogs are blood kin to pookas. Leastwise my experience would suggest as much. This might well explain how dogs are a lot like people in a great many ways. Tom Quinn knew that. Mike and Amy learned it. I still learn it more and more each day.

I wasn't being fanciful when I suggested that you might go and ask Sparky about pookas. You very well might, and he very well might answer you, if he were so inclined. And, whether or not he would be so inclined would be a matter of the pooka within him, to be sure. They are like that. Dogs and pookas, that is, about the people that they might be inclined to talk to. You have to let them sniff your hand first.

Mike and Amy will tell you that, too. Did I tell you that they're engaged? Of course, they have to finish college first. Anyway, just sit a spell. I'll tell you our story and about how I came to know these things. It all began with Tom Quinn and his dog, Pete. And then, of course, there's Rooster.

Would you like a glass of chocolate milk?

Let's see. Where to begin? Where is my guitar?

Okay, here we go…a cowboy song.

Get along little doggie
Get along little doggie
It's a long, long trail
And we ride to the end

Get along little doggie
When the trail is over
We'll be riding again

Get along little doggie
Get along little doggie
There are stars in the night sky
To show us the way

Get along little doggie
We'll be riding the trail
Till the break of day

Get along little doggie
Get along little doggie
Over mountains and hills
Across rivers and streams

Get along little doggie
The trail we're riding
Is made of hopes and dreams

That is a cowboy song, and the doggies that they sing of are cattle calves. Our story is the story of the canine kind; of the English pointers and English setters that compete in the sport of American field trials, a kind of cowboy game; and of a flop-eared, yellow-eyed, orange dog name Rooster, who wished to play along. If there is fantasy in it, well that is what hopes and dreams are made of.

PART ONE

PETE

ONE

Back in those days they still culled litters.

Tom Quinn was a field trialer. Mike, and I met him long after a fall from a sabotaged saddle broke his hip and removed him from competition, when he was a grizzled old man and arthritis hobbled his walk so that he could only continue training his pointing dogs with the help of his brother, Liam, or his niece, Amy, or anyone else who might show up at his grounds with the idea of getting a handling education in return for some field work. A big part of what I am telling you is the story of Tom Quinn.

One early summer, sometime in the early fifties, when he was of an age to leave home, Tom and his duffle bag boarded a Greyhound bus in Springfield, Massachusetts. The bus would take him cross country to the Drift Fields of North Dakota and to the summer training grounds of Duke Arness, a champion handler and breeder of English pointers.

Tom had learned of field trialing from his uncle, Will, who had once dabbled in the sport recreationally. The notion of wearing leather chaps and following, on horseback, far-ranging braces of pointing dogs across Dakota pheasant fields or Oklahoma quail haunts appealed to a New England boy raised on Autry and Cassidy picture shows. For Tom, though, even more seductive than the leathered charm of a cowboy, was the allure of working with pointing dogs.

In this, the two occupations are well joined. A field trial pointer is not unlike the cowboy of the old West. He is a range rover, living a hard and fast life. On game, he is a gun slinger in profile; a shootist, his sinuous muscles taut as a trigger pull, his tail at high noon. The English might compare their pointer to a chess rook, mightily moving in straight lines to check its game, but in this country, the pointer is a cowboy.

On his arrival in North Dakota, Tom was met by Duke and his son, Buck, a sandy-haired young man about Tom's age, riding shotgun in Duke's red Ford pick-up truck, and by the lanky Tall Charlie Hinkle, Buck's crony, who rode in the truck bed where Tom would also ride; these boys, along with Duke's long-time scout, Fuzz Conklin, who was back at the camp, made up Duke's crew. Introductions were exchanged, and Duke inquired of Tom's uncle.

"Uncle Will's fine," said Tom, shaking Duke's hand, "and he sends his regards with his thanks for giving me this opportunity."

"Think nothing of it," said Duke. Then turning to his son, who was still seated in the truck, "We can always use the help, can't we Buck?"

"Sure," Buck replied through the cab of the truck, with a hint of insincerity evidenced by a twisted smile and a sly glance toward Tall Charlie, who stood outside the truck by the passenger window. Tall Charlie returned Buck's glance with a gapped tooth grin. Buck and Charlie doubted the Massachusetts boy's worth. Proving himself would not be easy for Tom.

The Drift Plains of North Dakota epically unfold in summertime shades of green and greenish-gold. In the wind, the tall plains grasses breathe with waves that lull the eye with their undulations. Flocks of clouds pasture in a sky the color of forget-me-nots. As the red Ford pick-up dustily rolled toward Duke's camp, Tom, his legs extended a bit uncomfortably in the back, took in his surroundings and felt the anticipation of new beginnings.

Fuzz Conklin was outside the graying and weather beaten bunk house, a black-eared pointer pup clamped in the crook of his right arm and several other black and whites scampering eagerly around his feet, it being meal time. "This here is Fuzz," said Duke with a wave.

"Yeah, cause he don't shave none too often," cracked Buck.

"Yeah, but he cain't grow no beard, neither," added Tall Charlie, his own face showing several days' growth.

Fuzz let go of the black-eared pup, and it ran off like its meal was elsewhere. "Go git 'im, Buck," pushed Fuzz. "You too, Charlie!" he snapped, and then he turned to shake hands with Tom, first wiping his own on his faded denim pants.

Charlie ran after the dog, which was not inclined to come when called. Buck, being the lazier of the two, hopped into the pickup truck, figuring that the pup couldn't be caught on foot. The pup's line was straight and vigorously fast for a young dog, but Buck soon got alongside. In the parallel movement of vehicle and dog, Buck opened his door, reached down out of the cab, and with one motion grabbed the pup by the scruff of its neck and hurled it roughly into the truck bed. The dog did not yelp.

TWO

"Let's go inside," Duke invited Tom, "I'll show you to your bunk. You can stow your duffle underneath."

The bunk house wasn't meant for much more than sleeping, except it also had a coal black cook stove and a rough-hewn, aged wooden table with some slat-back wooden chairs, also worn to a beating. An old, faded white Frigidaire ice box sat humming in one corner. There was some unpainted wood shelving for a cupboard, prominent on it was a somewhat tarnished bronze trophy of a dog on point.

"That's from my first Invitational," explained Duke. "I've got others back home, but the first one is my constant inspiration. This sport can be dang fool frustratin' at times."

Buck swaggered into the bunk house. Charlie shuffled in behind him and sniffled. Each was met with a disapproving stare from Duke. "Buck, you and Charlie know I don't like you running down dogs from the truck," he scolded, rising to his full height. "That dog could've run 'neath a tire, or ya could've hurt its leg or somethin' when you threw 'im inta the bed like that." Duke's anger was evident in his truncated speech.

"Aw Pah," drawled Buck, hunched at the shoulders, his shirt tail untucked, his hair mussed, "we're probably gonna cull that pup anyhow; it don't have no manners, and its style ain't nothin' special no how. He'll never earn no prize money, that's fer sure."

Charlie hung his head with the guilt of a co-conspirator. He looked up at Duke from beneath the bill of his stained and tattered red cap. He forced his lips from their lackey's smirk into the frown of a feigned contrition, and then he sniffled, shuffled and turned slightly away so as not to meet Duke's piercing grey eyes. He coughed a smoker's cough behind a loose fist.

"That's no never mind," chided Duke, "I don't like it, and that's reason enough for you boys."

You can see forever in North Dakota, and that's appropriate, because the sun breaks so very, very far, far away. When it breaks, casting rose, cirrus wisps overhead, it rouses the pups and stirs the horses. The air is chilly fresh and the day is sunrise new, and the work begins at the camp with the reveille of horses, dogs and men.

"We start with the older dogs," Duke informed Tom that following morning, "gives 'em the greater likelihood of bird work."

There were three older dogs; "shooting dogs" they're called, as that is the name of the field trial stake in which they compete. Then four "derby" dogs and five pups from Duke's October litter, the black-eared pup among them. The latter were to be evaluated for their potential and for possible competition in the coming fall, in "futurities" and puppy stakes. Other dogs would come and go over the course of the summer, being brought or sent by their owners for training or conditioning under Duke's tutelage.

The dogs were kenneled in individual crates on a gray, one-horse, wooden wagon driven by Fuzz Conklin. Duke and the boys rode horseback, Tom on a sorrel mare.

"You can handle a horse, Tom?" asked Duke.

"I can," Tom replied with confidence. Buck and Tall Charlie were suspicious, one elbowing the other with a snicker. But Tom had had experience with horses, and in that regard Buck and Tall Charlie would get no pleasure in seeing him embarrassed.

They rode only a short while, stopping at an expanse of Drift Prairie terrain, level for the most part, but with small hills and coulees and covered with tall wild grains and patches of greenish yellow scrub thickets and otherwise dotted with isles of poplar, box elder and birch, all along adjacent fallow fields of the stubby remains of last year's corn, the color of ocean driftwood; it was land that Duke knew was likely to hold pheasants.

Each end of a link of chain was staked into the ground not far from the wagon, and then the dogs were leashed at intervals along this chain, forming a "string of dogs," which was a method of their socialization as well as their restraint. An older dog might sit mannerly on the chain; a younger one might fidget, fuss, and bark, but the pups would yip and pull and fight their captivity until wearied by it.

"This here is ringneck pheasant country, although there may also be grouse and prairie chickens hereabout," Duke told Tom as he chained a dog to the string. "The pheasant is a wily bird that won't generally hold ground, least not with a pointing dog atop it," he added, "so it's a good bird for a dog to get wisdom on. Besides, often a pheasant'll run a bit 'fore it flushes to flight, and so the wizened dog will learn to relocate, which is a good talent for a field dog to have." Tom nodded an uncertain understanding as he reached to pet the black-eared pup.

"Go grab Ike, that end dog there, and bring 'im up here to me," Duke told Tom as he walked to his horse. "Bring your mare, too," he added.

Tom did as Duke directed. With his left hand grasping the dog's collar as the dog struggled to break free, and with the reins of the mare in his right hand, Tom stood by Duke. Buck and Tall Charlie waited nearby astride their horses, passing a joke or some other reason for amusement between them, likely at Tom's expense. Duke turned to Tom, "When I tell you, just let Ike go and command the dog to hie on."

"*Hie on!*"

Thus cast, the pointer broke away powerfully, like a thoroughbred out of a racing gate at a country fair. Arrow straight at first, but then angling slightly to the right, it covered better than a furlong before Tom had turned to mount his mare. The others were already a dozen yards or so ahead, although at a walking gait. Their pace would quicken as the dog's speed and angle required.

THREE

Before long, Ike was gone from view. Tall Charlie pulled out of the group to scout. "Dog's on point," he soon hollered from a distance. Duke followed the call with Buck and Tom along. Ahead, in the stubble of the cornfield, Ike stood staunchly on point, muscles pulsing, tail held high and ram rod straight, his left foreleg crooked. Duke dismounted and slowly approached to flush. Ike needed no cautioning, or "whoaing," as it is called.

When Duke saw the pheasant, he hurried his pace. The bird did not wait to be prodded and quickly fluttered to wing. The crack of Duke's blank gun followed, Ike holding steady to wing and shot. Duke collared the dog away at a right angle to the bird's flight and then released it to begin the hunt anew. "*Hie on!*" So commanded, the dog continued its race with an obvious intensity of purpose. Repeated finds were marked by staunch points and flushed birds taking flight with screeched cackles, followed by the pop of Duke's gun.

When time was called, the dog was collared on a long lead, which was passed to Buck, and the party rode back to the wagon. "The only training with these older dogs," Duke told Tom during the return, "is in the correction of faults; busting birds, breaking on the shot, that kind of thing. For these older dogs we're more concerned with their conditioning. Today we ran Ike for about forty minutes; by the end of the camp, he'll be running for far better than two hours, full out, with a good run still in him to spare."

"The measure of a field trial dog is in his nose, his style, and his stamina. We can't teach nose, 'cause it is whatever the good Lord give 'im. But, we'll put him on as many birds as we can or nature provides. Style too is something the dog's either got or he ain't. All we can do with style is teach the dog what it needs to do so as to make a proper presentation—that is, run always to the front, never behind, and be staunch and steady on point to the wing and the shot. That's what we'll work on with the derby dogs. As for the puppies, we're just gonna see what they got . . . do a little steadiness on those pigeons we got cooped, or such other birds as the pups might find if we take 'em afield. Mostly we'll just introduce 'em to this game of ours and see how they take to it."

They worked the two remaining older dogs, each rendering far-ranging runs, turning appropriately into wind-carried scent; searching likely cover of copse, scrub, and dead corn; and giving finished performances with each found bird. They took up the derby dogs next. These needed handling on their birds. Buck and Tall Charlie would approach the dog when it made point, cautioning it a bit too harshly for Duke's liking, then one or the other would collar the dog to steady it as the other flushed the bird and made shot. If the dog pulled to break away, it was disciplined, again sometimes too harshly for Duke, and Duke would let the boys know it.

"There's no need to whoop a dog with a flushing stick just 'cause it wants to chase a bird," Duke scolded. "That's its instinct. We don't want to break the dog's desire. Better to put it back on its point, calm it down and then let it know that you'd appreciate better behavior." The boys would look toward the ground while being scolded, but that didn't fully hide their insubordinate smirks.

"Those dogs need manners, Pa," Buck replied, "some more than others. We're just teaching 'em the business end . . . gettin' their respect is all." Duke hadn't the inclination to argue. "Just do like I says," he growled.

Lastly the pups were run on long check cords and guided to where a clipped-wing pigeon was planted among shrubs or within tall grasses. The pups would naturally establish a tentative point upon catching scent but then begin to creep and have to be restrained. One of the boys would then go and pick up the crippled pigeon, toss it into the air away from the pup, and fire off a shot from his blank gun, the dog pulling hard to chase the bird as it fell, futilely flapping its remaining wing feathers. The handler would let go of the check cord, and the pup would pounce excitedly, hungrily, upon the disabled bird. Buck and Tall Charlie seemed to enjoy the mayhem. Tom only understood its brutal pragmatism.

Of the pups, the black-eared one fell to Tom to handle, likely because the others felt that the pup held no promise; it was unruly, its tail curved and angled at eleven o'clock, but it was a strong and vigorous dog, full with the desire of a desperately hungry forager. The pup did not want to be befriended and would not readily yield to command. Yet, Tom refused to adopt the cruel methods of Buck and Tall Charlie. He persisted in an effort to handle the dog with a tempered patience. Duke did not intervene; perhaps because he, too, had given up on the pup, or maybe because he felt that the unyielding dog afforded the boy from Massachusetts a necessary education.

FOUR

In that way, the summer continued. The days with the dogs afield were followed by nights sitting round the bunk house table or out under the North Dakota night sky, vast, violet, and star filled. Tom believed Fuzz Conklin when Fuzz told him that there were more stars in North Dakota than Massachusetts because the North Dakota sky was bigger.

Buck and Tall Charlie frequently left camp for town and a saloon called Musties. Tom went with them only rarely, when Duke and Fuzz would also go, usually on a Saturday night. Mostly Tom preferred the camp and the tales and histories that Duke or Fuzz would tell.

"Field trialing is not merely a sport," Duke once remarked. "It's a culture unto itself. The personages, by which I mean to include the dogs, even the horses, are like the characters in old story books, even like those of some epic poetries, though I figure most would be found in the pages of a Western dime novel, if only by similarity of name."

Tom would listen attentively when Duke recounted his acquaintances and their adventures, aided in his faded memory by Fuzz's own admittedly uncertain recollections. But, Duke often chided, "Keep in mind, boy, this is not an easy game. It is a hard competition, and there are those few, sufferin' of greed or otherwise ornery, who would not compete fairly, or would use trickery, and you've got to be wary of them. You'll know them 'cause their ways take a toll on their features, so that they look like the rascals that they truly are."

As the days and nights ran their course with repeated similarity, there was but one other instance worth special mention. On a late-July day, when Tom had the black-eared pup out on its braided lead, the pup slipped its collar, as it had not been correctly buckled, and bolted to its freedom. Tom ran to his horse and was quickly mounted, but the dog had gone from sight, being last seen a ways off, cresting a small hill. Tom spurred his mare to a gallop and atop the rise espied the still-running pup a good half mile out. He gave chase.

The challenge did not unnerve Tom. To the contrary, he felt an edgy excitement and a previously unknown ambition within the wind of the mare's gallop. He was closing on the dog, when it suddenly stopped, as if a wall had risen before it. A point!

Still yards away, Tom dismounted to approach the dog on foot. The black-eared pup showed a staunchness and intensity that it had not exhibited when at the end of a training lead. It turned its head only slightly, in acknowledgement of Tom's presence. It did not flinch or show any inclination to creep.

Tom voiced a hushed caution, "Whoa boy, easy boy," as he sought the bird that compelled the end of the dog's run. The ringneck was strutting in scrub well ahead of the pup's point. It took wing with a screech as Tom neared. To Tom's surprise, the pup did not chase, but stood firm, studying the bird's flight, even when Tom made shot. More surprisingly, the dog remained still as Tom reached to slip on its collar. With that accomplished, Tom hugged the pup and petted and praised it mightily, "Good dog, good, good dog." He mounted his horse with the pup under his right arm and rode back to the wagon with the pup across the mare's saddle. "Good dog, good, good dog," he repeated.

A short distance from the dog's point, purple spikes of dotted lazy star liatris pierced through the yellowing prairie grasses. A blue butterfly fluttered among the flowers, and came to rest as Tom dismounted, observing all that followed with stilled curiosity. When the dog and rider had gone from sight over a knoll, the butterfly again busied herself among the blooms, humming a soft Celtic lay.

FIVE

I asked Sparky if the black eared pup, having just freed himself from the fetter of his collar, would really have stopped mid-escape to point a pheasant in the vastness of the North Dakota prairie. Sparky said, "That puppy couldn't help but point that pheasant.

"That's the dharma of the pointing dog. It has no choice in the matter. A pointing dog is hotwired to point game, be it a pheasant in a prairie, or a grouse in some timbers, or a partridge in a pear tree. A pointing dog encounters game and the dog locks up in a staunch, flesh pulsating, ribs protruding point that exclaims to the handler 'there!' He's got no choice in the matter whatsoever. It's pointing dog dharma.

"And, that black eared pup didn't just stumble across that pheasant in the vast emptiness of the grasslands. That pup was drawn, like iron is drawn to a magnet, by the sniff of the bird upon the prairie breezes. The dog could no more ignore the draw of the bird's scent than it could chose not to halt its run and lock up on point. Dharma, like I said.

"On the other hand," Sparky continued, pacing about contemplatively, "what the pointing dog does after making its point *is* a matter of choice. That's where you can see how dogs can be a lot like people at times. If a person doesn't want to do something, well then, they don't have to do it, and there isn't much about which a person has no choice of doing or not doing. Dogs can be heady and uncompliant, just like people. Look at me," he allowed with a snicker. Truth be told, he is a mischievous little imp. Downright bratty, Jan says.

"So, the pointing dog," he continued after quickly looking back over his shoulder towards the kitchen, "having been obliged to point the game, isn't necessarily obliged to hang around and wait for a handler to come and flush the game, or to stand his point when the bird takes to wing, or at the shot. Dang if it does, too, it being a predator. For the most part, that's something that has to be trained, steadiness to flush, wing and shot. That's what folks like Duke Arness do, train pointing dogs to be steady to flush, wing and shot, although not harshly, like you heard Buck might do.

"But, once in a while, you'll get a dog that somehow knows and values its relationship with its handler. Such a dog inherently understands that it is part of a team, part of a pack, as it once was long ago in its evolution. It's genetic. In canine sport and in the wolf pack, that's called cooperation. But, more than mere cooperation as among a pack of wolves, when it comes to humans and dogs, it is companionship.

"That black eared puppy, when he stood staunch and still as Tom approached, and stood staunch and still at the flush and shot, and then allowed Tom to collar him and carry him astride the mare back to camp, that black eared pup made a choice; it chose companionship with the young Tom Quinn. That's not dharma. That's karma.

"That's what that butterfly saw as it watched from amid the liatris. There are more things among and about woodland creatures than appearances might suggest. He took an interest in Tom Quinn, the butterfly did. Took an interest in the way the boy and the dog somehow came together, in their karma. Later on you'll see how…" but, Sparky didn't finish. He abruptly turned and scampered into the kitchen and across the floor to where Jan was preparing his dinner. Sparky is a companionable conversationalist; but, eating comes first. I suspect that must be his dharma, eating, especially treats, the little imp.

I'm not as attuned as Sparky to such notions as dharma and karma. I suspect Sparky must have learned something of those fanciful ideas from the pooka. Still, having heard as much from Sparky, I reckon that dharma explains a lot about what happened with Rooster that day when Mike first took him to Crooked Creek and they met Tom Quinn so many years later. And, I'll venture that karma probably explains what happened that same day when Mike and Amy met for the first time. When we get to that part of our story, let me know your thoughts, or how you feel. They are fanciful notions, after all.

SIX

The idea that Tom had possibly found companionship in the black eared pup did not sit well with Buck Arness. Field trial dogs were not meant for companionship. They were meant for competition. They were meant to be indifferent and devil-may-care, meant to be "hell bent." Buck was hard on his dogs, and he would cull the weak. He was thinking Tom was weak, Tom and his black eared pup.

Buck and Hinkle schemed and thought to frustrate Tom's learning. Little things, a loose collar that a dog might slip, a loose saddle cinch that might force Tom to dismount and re-buckle along the trail, causing him to lag and be tardy, and nuisance tasks that served no purpose other than to bother; little things that small minded boys found amusement in, like teases in school, like bullies. But, Tom was not to be undone. Buck and Tall Charlie could not nettle a weakness in Tom Quinn, and soon they would learn of his strength. It happened in mid-August; on a night when Tom accepted Buck's invitation to go to Musties after a long, hot and thirsty day pursuing wayward dogs.

In a town as old as the Wild West, Musties was an Old West combination eatery and saloon, with an old, oaken bar separated from a dining area of old, round, oaken tables with red checkered table cloths by a half-wall partition of old slats of dirtied Ponderosa pine. The place had a gun slinger history not too long past, and bullet holes still pockmarked walls, ceiling and floors. A room clearing brawl was not an uncommon occurrence even still.

As I mentioned earlier, Tom was ordinarily not inclined to go with Buck and Tall Charlie on their trips to Musties, a place where minors might yet drink beer with a low alcohol content or near beer, as it was called. But, this night Duke and Fuzz Conklin had gone upstate to return a dog to its owner after the dog had twisted a leg in a gopher hole and gone limp. So, Tom chose not to stay alone at the cabin, especially as there would be no dinner. While Tom, Buck and Tall Charlie sat eating a meatball stew in the dining area, two young local men came in. They greeted Buck and Charlie and were introduced to Tom as an "eastern dude come to learn dog wrangling."

"This is Robby Strand and Alvie Ahlgren," said Buck. They're local boys, born and raised." Shaking hands, Tom stated his pleasure, "Glad to meet you." The taller boy, Robby Strand, returned the smile, while the other nodded in agreement, "Same here," and then they made their way to the bar. "They've worked dogs with us from time to time," Buck told Tom, "handy with a pheasant gun, which is how they make their living during the season, guiding out-of-towners on hunts," he continued. "Duke has sold them dogs in the past."

After a moment, Buck and Hinkle left the table to have drinks at the bar with Strand and Ahlgren. Tom sat and finished his stew and then got up and went to the men's room, which was off to the back of the saloon behind the bar. As Tom stood at the urinal, Strand came in with Ahlgren, who roughly shouldered Tom so as to squeeze by on his way to the stall. When Tom objected, Strand shoved him from behind and jeered, "Ain't enough room in these parts for eastern dudes," and he laughed and Ahlgren cawed. "Don't need to crowd me, guys," Tom responded somewhat apologetically, but Strand pushed him a second time, and then Ahlgren shoved him, saying "No room, dude." Tom didn't want trouble with the local boys and turned to leave, but both boys barred his way, Strand with his arms across his chest and Ahlgren wearing a glassy-eyed and challenging smirk.

Tom's dad had died when Tom was 10, and his Uncle Will had helped his mom to raise him upright. Uncle Will had just returned home a decorated marine from the war in the Pacific, and he was intent to make sure that his nephew could fend for himself in an intemperate world. Tom brought a strong right fist to the left side of Strand's head, causing him to fall against the urinal toward Ahlgren, who pushed him aside so as to reach at Tom. But, Ahlgren was too slow; for no sooner had Tom walloped Strand, then he brought his left to Ahlgren's midsection doubling him, and then a right atop his lowered head, dropping him to the ground at Strand's feet. Strand leaned dizzily against the urinal, gawking unsurely at Tom through a swollen left eye. Tom turned and left the room, not saying another word. Uncle Will had taught Tom well.

Buck and Tall Charlie were standing at the bar when Tom came out of the men's room. Tom said to Buck, "We should go, now." Buck complained that it was early and that he was not inclined to leave so soon; but, just as Tom grabbed his arm to pull him towards the exit door, he saw a battered Strand and weak-legged Ahlgren come out of the men's room, and he understood. "Let's go," he said to Hinkle. Tall Charlie downed the last of his near beer, wiped his lips with his sleeve, gave a quizzical look towards Strand and Ahlgren, and followed Buck and Tom out.

Tom rode in the back of the pick-up truck on the ride back to camp. There were no words exchanged between him and Buck or Charlie. What had happened at Musties was simply understood. Tom Quinn was not to be culled.

SEVEN

The summer of training ended with an early September full moon, a vast moon in a vast North Dakota sky, gold upon violet. That night in the bunk house, Tom sat at the table discussing his future plans with Duke, while Fuzz busied himself with end-of-camp chores. Buck and Tall Charlie came in, brushing dirt off their faded Wrangler jeans, Tall Charlie slapping his thighs with his cap.

"That ditch dug?" Duke asked them.

"Yes sir," Buck replied.

Duke reached up to remove his rim-fire rifle from its rack on the wall. He slid the gun across the table to Tom.

"Tom," he began, "This here is a hard and difficult sport, hard and difficult; all the more so with the dog breeding and all. It just ain't easy on either the body or the spirit, and it requires some things that cut against the grain of what we might otherwise prefer as good and compassionate men," he said somewhat somberly.

"We can't keep all of them pups we got with us, Tom. Heck, if I had to keep all the dogs that I've bred over the years, I'd have hundreds, and it just ain't practical to keep and feed so many animals. Some of them pups just ain't field trial material, and that's just the facts of life, Tom. We gotta cull that litter . . . keep only the two that we figure got potential. The other three we have to dispose of, Tom. You're new at this, boy . . . but you gotta learn this part of it just as much as the other parts. It's a hard and difficult sport, Tom, hard and difficult."

Tom looked down at the gun with a shocked awareness of what was being asked of him. "Mr. Arness, I just can't do that, sir. I just don't think that I can do that. It's not something I've come here prepared for . . . not something I anticipated at all. I appreciate all that you've done for me, Mr. Arness, I really do, and I hope that I can repay you someday; but, sir, I need you not to make me do what you ask."

16

Duke Arness looked toward Fuzz Conklin, who slowly shook his head and then returned to his sweeping. "All right, boy, I understand," he said. Then he turned to Buck. "You and Charlie go tend to it. Go on." Buck, sneering at Tom, picked the rifle up from the table, then turned, slapped Tall Charlie on the back, and the two of them shuffled towards of the door with a sniffle, snort and a haw.

"Wait," called Tom uneasily.

"Mr. Arness," Tom worriedly turned to Duke, "That black-eared pup… is he among the culls?" Duke nodded, "he is, Tom." "Mr. Arness, I'd like to keep that pup, sir. I'll pay you a fair price for 'im, if I can send you the money when I get home. I've taken to that dog. I can work 'im and maybe he'll do all right, at least by me."

Duke put his hand on Tom's shoulder and searched his eyes. He looked to Fuzz, who nodded, and then he turned to Buck. "Save that black-eared dog for Tom, here." However, Buck did not pay him any mind as he and Charlie sauntered out of the cabin, letting the screen door slam behind them. Duke turned back to Tom. "Tell your uncle, Will, that I said hello. He's a fine man." Then, he, too, went outside.

Soon rifle shots were heard . . . two in rapid succession, then a third a moment later.

Perhaps we should just pause here for a moment. I'd like to tell you something of the early history of the American field trial. We'll come back. We'll come back to Tom's story in a moment. There's more.

EIGHT

The bottomlands and pine ridges of Western Tennessee are considered the birthplace of the American field trial. The town of Grand Junction, not too far east of Memphis, is the home of The National Bird Dog Museum and The Field Trial Hall of Fame. For enthusiasts, it is an inspiring facility, a monument to the history of the sport and to the dogs, handlers, trainers and judges that challenged the upland courses that the historian, Everett M. Skehan, has called the *Fields of Glory*.

At the Hall of Fame, you'll learn of Rip Rap, considered the first English Pointer to win a recognized field trial championship in the United States, besting the competition at the Eastern Field Trial Club's Championship in High Point, North Carolina, on November 21, 1892. Up until then, the champions of the sport had all been English Setters, like Tom's Queen, of whom I'll tell you more a little later. Notably, it has been said that Rip Rap won his championship in the strongest setter year that the sport had seen up until that time.

And you'll learn, too, of Becky Broom Hill, the pointer female whose perfect manners, natural instincts to hunt all the right covers, always to the front and never to the rear, and whose strength of endurance in championship meets, which often ran as long as four hours back then, enabled her to tally the greatest record in the first seventy-five years of the sport, with a percentage of first place finishes that has never yet been equaled among dogs with more than thirty field trial placements.

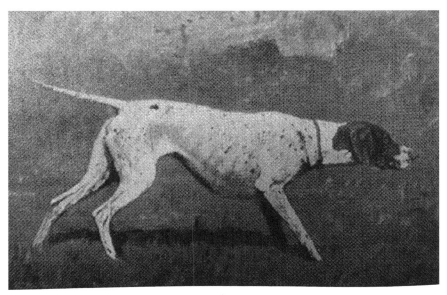

Three-Time National Champion Becky Broom Hill

Included in Becky Broom Hill's twenty-two first place wins are two Manitoba Championships, a National Free-for-All Championship, and three National Championships. She was the first female to win the National Free-for-All Championship, which she did just one week after her controversial win over the champion setter, Eugene's Ghost, in the 1922 National. In doing so, she became the first female to capture the country's two premier field trial championships back-to-back.

In beating Eugene's Ghost, Becky Broom Hill also bested one of the more colorful trainers and handlers of the early field trial era, Hall of Famer, Jim Avent, who had handled the Hall of Fame setter, Count Gladstone IV, to an even more controversial win of the very first National Championship in 1896.

James M. Avent

Avent was known as the "Fox of Hickory Valley." It is said that his nickname was well-earned, and he surely looked the part, with a slender face extended by thin nose pointed over a bushy auburn mustache. He was a brash competitor, the kind of man to have pet bears staked out in the frontage of his sporting lodge, the Rustic Inn, in Hardeman County, Tennessee, just a few miles from Grand Junction.

Avent is reputed to have been obsessed with winning at any cost, and legend relates a number of instances of his shady tactics, such as having disguised and illegal scouts posted at critical locations along field trial courses, out of sight of the gallery and judges. These co-conspirators might then aid or favor an Avent dog by interfering with its brace mate's point, or by running the brace mate off course. As you'll hear me tell a bit later, Jim Avent would have met his match in Buck Arness.

Hobart Ames is also enshrined in the Field Trial Hall of Fame. Ames judged an unequalled thirty National Championships. More to his undying honor and memory, he gave to the sport a perpetual home for the National Championship, his 18,000 acre Ames Plantation in western Tennessee. It is he who gave the sport the so called Amesian Standard, a statement of the ideals to be sought in the judgment of field trial dogs, some being as Duke tried to explain them to Tom that summer in North Dakota. He was a man widely renowned and highly regarded for his uncompromised integrity and his unflagging commitment to the sport of the American Field Trial. Among the early pioneers of the sport, Hobart Ames is rightly honored above all others.

From William J. Allen to William Ziegler, Jr. and from Air Pilot to Wrapup, there are over 260 men, women, and dogs enshrined in the Field Trial Hall of Fame, each a sporting star of merit and acclaim.

In 1973, Duke Arness would join them.

Now, where were we? Oh yeah, we just left Tom and the cull of the litter.

NINE

Tom took the black-eared pup home with him when he left North Dakota.

A young man and a pup can fairly be called an intention of nature. There is a bond between them that goes beyond what is ordinarily thought of as companionship. There is trust and faith and a mutual dependency unlike what human companions might share. When the dog and man are called to sport, as in the case of field trialing, they are teammates. Leaving North Dakota, Tom and the pup traveled in companionship. Soon they would be a team.

The American horseback field trial is likely one of the oldest organized sports in the United States, reliably dating back to 1874. In venues from the wooded fields, abandoned orchards and wildlife management areas in the northeast, to the plantations in the Deep South, and across to the prairies and ranches of the West, from Texas to Manitoba, Canada, on virtually every weekend of the year, in all kinds of weather, handlers, judges and spectators, horses, and strings of pointing dogs gather for the competition. The stakes are local or regional or national in challenge, run on quail or pheasant, partridge, grouse, or prairie chickens or any combination thereof that the habitat affords. Even the woodcock may come into play in the brush knolls, cedar fens and alder runs of New England or the Lake States.

The competition is drawn and run in two-dog braces; however, the winner is not judged merely against its brace mate, but also against all competitors in the meet. At the start of the stake, the handlers collar their spirited and eager dogs to the break before the mounted judges and a mounted, marshaled gallery, the handler's own mounts nearby at the ready. The dogs are cast "hie on" in parallel lines that widen or cross, depending on the course or the cover or on a dog's inclinations or its scent of game. Should the dogs' paths come together when one is standing on point, the first dog's point is to be honored by the second, the failing of which is a fault and a disqualification. All the while the dogs are evaluated on the energy and strength of their races, the number of birds found, the style of their points, and their steadiness at the flush and shot, the judges looking for what is best described as the class of the meet.

In some contests, particularly those of national importance, there may be as many as fifty or more dogs involved, with the competition extending over three or more days. These are busy days from dawn to dusk. The evenings are gatherings of weathered and ride-worn men and women, tired and lathered horses, dogs still too high strung to bed down, camp fires, meals, and socialization such as only arises in the culture of the sporting dog. At the end the handlers crate up their dogs; trailer up their horses and tack; pack up their pickups, campers and tents; and head to the next venue, their departure evoking an image not unlike that of the wagon trains of the old West.

Tom would join this society, this culture of men and dogs, and the competition of the American field trial. He had spent the summer learning and training with one of the best. There would be much more to learn, experience being the teacher that it is reputed to be, and Tom would learn well. Later on, he'd share that knowledge with others, like my son, Mike. At this point in our story, though, he was at the break away, eager for the cast, and with a youth's energy and a greenhorn's ambition to be "hie on" over a new course of unfamiliar but vividly imagined terrain.

TEN

Tom was met at home by his ma and his Uncle Will, who both wondered at the pup. "Mr. Arness gave him to me," Tom explained. "I saved 'im from the cull. He's a good dog, Uncle Will, and I plan to run 'im in some puppy stakes this fall. He's called Pete, but I think that he was registered by Mr. Arness as Duke's Tenderfoot, which I like pretty much; but Pete's a good name. The way he gives you a hard time, you're always saying 'for Pete's sake,' but I think I can make a good field trial dog of 'im. He's got desire and ranges real nice. His tail ain't perfect, and he didn't show good manners, which was why Mr. Arness was gonna put 'im down in the cull. He'll do for my first dog, though. What do you think, Uncle Will?"

The pup excitedly leapt at, up, and on Uncle Will as he bent forward to make his greetings. "Good muscles, on him, huh?" he asked rhetorically. "I venture he can run well, but you know style is just about everything, Tom. I'll have to see him on birds. Anyway, I'll give you a hand as you like. Pete, huh? All right, Pete, we'll have some fun, I imagine. It's been a while since I followed a trial dog. Good. I'm in." He turned to Tom's ma. "What do you think, Martha?"

Mrs. Quinn petted the dog, looked warmly at Tom, and smiled that uncertain smile of a mother whose son is showing his first beard, and said, "You boys go and have your fun. Just don't expect me to pick up after you. Tom, you come in and eat. Tell me about North Dakota." She turned to the house.

Tom turned to Uncle Will. "Mr. Arness says hello. He's a good man, and I learned a lot from him. I suppose I troubled him in the end, when I couldn't cull the litter, but I think he understood. His son, Buck and another fellow, Tall Charlie, they had no scruples about culling the pups. I don't think that I'll understand it ever. But, they seemed to. It seemed like they even took some ill pleasure in it. But Mr. Arness didn't. He was bothered by it, I'm sure. It was a difficult thing, he said. Although it had to be done, he said. I saved Pete, though. He's a good dog, he is." And Tom reached down and scruffed the back of the dog's head behind its one black ear. He gave the dog a tender pat on the shoulder and a teasing push, and Pete leapt at him playfully. "He's a good dog, alright. Ain't ya, Pete?" He picked the dog up and their eyes communicated.

Tom's ma called to him from the porch door. "You come on in now and wash and I'll have some dinner for you, meatloaf and potatoes, green beans from the garden. We had a good garden this summer. Don't know what I have for dog food, though. He'll have to eat some bread 'til tomorrow, when I can go to the market. I'll mix some gravy in the bread. He'll like that, I bet."

"Bet he will," said Tom as he stepped up on to the porch carrying the dog under one arm. He reached the door and gave his mom a kiss on the cheek. She looked back at Uncle Will and shook her head with a soft smile of submission. "Now, where's that younger brother of yours?" she asked abstractedly. "He's gotten pretty independent of late for a boy just ten years old. Liam!" she called. "Tom's home, come to dinner." She rang a dinner bell and heard the boy's "comin' ma" then, "ho Tom, ho, I'm coming."

ELEVEN

A field trial dog is a kennel dog. Kept outside, its existence is Spartan. Like a cowboy herding steer to market or tending a remote range, the field trial dog knows no luxuries.

Not so for Pete, though.

Tom's mom wasn't inclined towards keeping a dog in the house, but Tom persisted. "I rescued him from the cull, ma. He and I have got this bond. I can't have him sleepin' outdoors. It was different in North Dakota, 'cause there were other dogs for him to sleep with. He'd be all alone here. He'll be all right sleepin' with Liam and me in our room. I promise."

"That dog causes me any trouble…and you and the dog will both sleep outside." She gave Liam a stern look, as if he were the cause of her consternation. Then she sighed and affectionately patted Tom's head with motherly resignation. Tom brushed back the hair that she mussed. Liam, holding Pete in his lap, just smiled and touched his cheek atop the black eared pointer's brow.

Of course, Pete, a pup used to having other pups to lie around with, wasn't about to sleep alone on a cold floor. Not that Tom minded the dog on the bed at his feet; it was when Pete bellied his way up to the head board that Tom would complain, although the dispute usually ended with a shared pillow.

With a pup in your room there is no sleeping late or lying about lazily in the morning. A dog needs early morning tending, and a field trial dog more so than most, as it is a high strung and energetic dog, not inclined to simply laze about all the day long, as you might envision a coon hound draped over the steps of a plantation house veranda.

So it was that each morning Tom and Pete were up and out of the house almost before first light. Getting Pete a run was paramount among Tom's considerations. Tom often took Pete to the nearby Crooked Branch Wildlife Management Area, Pete riding with Tom in the cab of Uncle Will's green Dodge pickup truck with the dented front fender and faded "I like Ike" bumper sticker.

Tom hadn't a horse back then, and at first he was concerned about his ability to trail his far ranging pup, but Pete never ran off, and though he would get to the far horizons, he would always turn to check on his young handler, returning or slowing to a patterned prowl so as to always keep Tom within sight, while nonetheless busily investigating likely bird cover.

Such cooperation is the epitome of hunting companionship, but dallying to maintain contact with a handler will fault a field trialer, whose race is judged by nearly reckless abandon to the front. Still, for young Tom this cooperation was a form of communication, and through it, an education as to the manner and mind of the sporting dog.

"It's not all instinct," he challenged Uncle Will when pressed, ceasing his chore and resting his rake against the barn wall. "At least not with Pete, it isn't. Pete reasons. I know it's true because he speaks to me. He communicates with me. It isn't just some dog doing what comes natural. If it is…then it's my nature, too."

"You just might be right, boy." Uncle Will replied, wiping a hand upon his denim slacks, "On both accounts."

TWELVE

In the early evening, Tom and Pete would sit out on the front porch. "Ol' Fuzz Conklin was right about the stars," Tom would often remark to no one other than himself and Pete. "There just aren't so many stars here in Massachusetts, as there were in North Dakota."

Those days in North Dakota grew ever more distant, but not so far as to be long gone. They were often recalled, especially Duke's tales, advice and admonitions.

"In all my years," Duke once told Tom, "I've seen the good and the bad in both men and dogs. This sport'll teach you life's ways more so than much else in the world.

"Men…well…they have the free will God supposedly give 'em, and that's said to explain their misbehavior on occasion. I can accept that, so long as I don't have to tolerate no misconduct towards me or mine.

"Dogs…well…you know, they're just free animals, period, until you put controls on 'em. In their freedom, you don't see much that is misbehavior, per se, because they mostly do what they do in their natural state of mind, and what's natural dog behavior can't rightly be called misbehavior, now can it?

"That said, I do recall hearing of one dog that you'd swear was being mischievous by intention. This dog…you can ask Fuzz about him, too…well he'd done things that you'd just know were not accidental, yet you'd shake your head that they might be done on purpose.

"For instance, he was thought to deliberately intimidate a brace mate on point so as to cause a blink or a break. Folks would say their dog was rock solid until he came along, and then something just went awry."

"That was that old red patch-eyed dog," Fuzz joined in. "He could make a scowl to scare a coyote."

"Just how that dog got that way is a puzzlement, but you can be sure a man was involved. Still, I never could understand an animal with a malicious intent." Duke continued.

"Well, we kept away from fire-headed dogs for a reason," Fuzz added. "Not just the orange spotted dog, like you mostly finds among the pointers, mind you, but a fire red, like the devil was bred in it. You say man, I say devil."

"There're devils among men," Duke responded, "and, I say the man would be the fault of a bad dog, red markings or black. That's my conclusion."

A shooting star crossed the purple Massachusetts night and Tom made a wish. Then he stroked and scruffed Pete's head, "There's no devil in you, Pete," he said as he rose up from the shadows of the moonlit porch to retire. Pete followed him off to bed.

THIRTEEN

Pete didn't turn out to be the star that Tom had hoped he'd be, but, then again, Tom didn't have any unrealistic expectations. Oh, Pete had his moments, and he had a couple of placements in local stakes. One stake, in particular, Tom, in his later years, often liked to relate, especially to youngsters. Unless you are a child, I suppose that you would hear it told with a bit of skepticism, born of the Irish twinkle of Tom's hazel eyes.

To hear old Tom tell of it, during a shooting dog stake in Pennsylvania (or wherever Tom might imagine it at the moment), Pete pointed a grouse (or a quail, if Tom imagined it occurred in Georgia), and Tom flushed. The bird flew hard and fast, straight up, without a sound, then suddenly turned and dived right down at Pete, like a hawk on prey, pecked Pete on the stout, and then flew off again, leaving Tom looking dumbfounded and the judges and the gallery laughing in stitches. But Pete held his stance staunch and proud, and for that he took home the blue ribbon, at least so says a twinkle-eyed Tom Quinn.

Those things just don't happen, of course, but Tom would like you to believe that they do. Tom believes that when a man and his dog are together, there is plenty of room for the fancies of fortune or for a bit of fantasy to play a part, like in the old Greek poems or in Shakespeare's comedies, or like the faeries or wee folks of old Irish myth. I'd suppose you'd have to agree with him, if you had had his experiences. And, that's what Pete was all about.

Pete gave a young Tom Quinn the experiences he wanted, the opportunities to ride and to compete and to learn, and if Tom found in these experiences a bit of fantasy, well that was Tom's nature. All the more so when a soft autumn breeze, on a blue sky day, swayed tall heather gray grasses and floated burnished fall leaves along the course of a shooting dog stake, as Tom followed his dog astride his mare and inhaled the wonder of it all. It was good air, intoxicating air, in a fanciful way.

Pete helped to feed Tom's imaginings, as the endeavor of sport might feed another's muscles. More important, though, Pete was the foundation on which the dream of Quinn's Kennel was built, and the sire of a number of litters, including the one that later produced Tom's most successful dog, Deputy, a black-eared dog just like his great granddad. Deputy might have been a National Champion, except for what had happened at the Invitational in 1976 when Tom met again with Buck Arness and Tall Charlie Hinkle after so many years. That day seemed to change the fall grasses from heather to a leaden gray and the burnished autumn leaves to rust brown. And, the light in Tom's eyes became more spark than twinkle, but Tom never fully lost the wonder of fantasy that Pete had nurtured. One day it would rekindle in a most fanciful way.

FOURTEEN

There is no one word to describe the hunt and race of a shooting dog, like you might say of a horse that it gallops or of an eagle that it soars. The shooting dog's race is seldom sufficiently described even by combining those images or by adding any number of adjectives or adverbs. You may often hear such colorful descriptions as "hell bent for leather" or "wing footed" or "sizzling afire." Such metaphors aid your imaginings. The shooting dog's race is swift, agile, and nimble, yet not like a jazz rift, because it is predatory. It is like sword fencing, like a rapier cutting the air in a purposeful attack on the field trial course.

From the time he graduated to a shooting dog, Tom's Deputy was slicing through the field trial courses of the Eastern states. His April win as a four-year-old in the Georgia Open qualified him for the Invitational to be held the following November in Alabama. He would arrive with a reputation for gritty determination exercised with almost reckless abandon. He had the endurance of forged steel and a swashbuckling style that he flaunted when he was on point. "*En garde*," he seemed to say, at least to hear Tom tell it, and he commanded the attention and admiration of all who saw him.

Buck and Tall Charlie had heard of Deputy. They were at the Invitational with their liver-and-white pointer, Bandit, winner of the Missouri Open. They searched out Tom, finding him by his pop-up camper, sitting with his brother, Liam.

Buck greeted him, "Long time, Tom. Hear you've got yourself a special dog. Deputy, is it? Heard of him, we have. Good dog, huh? How've ya been?" He and Tall Charlie extended their hands in greeting. They were gnarled and leathery hands, darkened by days in the sun, dirty beneath the nails.

"Liam, this here is Buck Arness and Charlie Hinkle . . . Tall Charlie," said Tom by way of introductions. "I spent a summer in North Dakota training with them and Buck's dad, Duke Arness. How is Duke? I heard he was inducted into the Hall of Fame."

"He's just fine, but he's retired. I'm running the dogs now. Here with my Bandit. Ya heard've 'im?"

"Can't say that I recall at the moment, but it's possible, I try to keep up with the goings on."

"Well, hey, we got some other folks to look up on. We'll catch ya later on. Maybe we'll get braced in the call back."

"Yeah, sure. See ya round. Good luck."

"Yeah, you, too."

"They look pretty rascally to me," said Liam to Tom after Buck and Tall Charlie had left. "They don't look too trustworthy. Are they good folks?"

"They're all right," replied Tom. "They had a rough way with dogs that I didn't much care for. I can't say that I ever had reason to distrust them, though. They do look kinda ornery, now that you mention it. This is a hard and difficult sport, Liam. That's what Mr. Arness used to tell me. I guess it can change some folks over time. He said that, too. But, that's their business. I don't think we'll have to pay them much mind, 'cept maybe if we get braced with them and their Bandit. But, that won't happen unless we're both called back for the finals. We'll see. Pass me a pop, please, Liam." Liam popped the top with a bottle opener and handed the orange soda to Tom.

Liam was not far amiss in his observations. Buck didn't have the character of his dad. More than just retire, Duke had merely stepped aside, giving up on Buck, and letting him go off on his own, hoping that maybe life's lessons would make a better man of him. But, Buck didn't take to any lessons very readily, particularly if they were a hindrance to the vulgarity of his ambition. He was impatiently hungry for success. It was the gnarling impatience of a wolf in the stomach that could only be sated with the piggishness of winning at any cost. Rather than take the slow and righteous path, he took a crooked road. It showed in his features . . . his and Tall Charlie's. Their unshaven, ash-gray faces, their shoulders hunched. Their carriage betrayed their chicanery. They were not above some roguish improprieties or troublesome, even harmful, mischief or hooliganism. Many in the sport were justly wary of them.

FIFTEEN

In his race on the second day, Deputy impressed the judges enough to be selected for the callback, he and five others, one of which was Buck's Bandit, with whom Deputy was paired for the first brace of the finals. The night before, Buck and Tall Charlie again visited with Tom and Liam.

"Well, we got you in the draw, Tom," said Buck. "It'll be a good run, our two dogs."

"Nice dog you got there, Tom," added Tall Charlie, "Likely to give Bandit a run fer his vittles. That black ear reminds me of that pup you took with you from camp that summer long ago, any relation?"

"Great grandson," replied Tom. "I suspect it'll be a good run, Lord willing. You know how those things go."

"Oh, we know, don't we, Charlie?"

"Yup."

"See you at the break, boys."

"Yeah, see ya."

"Liam."

"Night."

The night was moonless. The stars were shaded by clouds. The camp fires had died down and the gathering had retired. You could not see so much as the shadow of the man with a knife bent on mischief in the dark. Later, in the gray light just before sunrise, the camp awoke and began the morning's preparations amid the sound of horse whinnies and barking dogs. The new day was overcast with dark gray clouds threatening to break.

The trial grounds were a blend of northeastern Alabama hills, hollows and flats; the dairy and wheat farm of Hiram Lee's plantation, with border acres of piney woods through which the trail would run before opening unto the fields of Indian grass, and the broomsedge, beggarweed, and pokeweed in which the quail coveyed. The break would be cast upon a tractor path at the base of the rise on which sat the manor house, the clearing wide enough for the gallery to ride as many as six abreast, and offering the dogs the option of searching amongst the shrubby understory of the bordering pines.

The gallery was gathered on horseback with the judges at the fore. The handlers approached with their dogs, Bandit and Deputy. These were collared to the break by their scouts, Tall Charlie and Liam, respectively, as Buck and Tom closely followed astride their Tennessee Walkers. The dogs were pantingly eager, rising up on their hind legs as they demanded to be let loose, giving their scouts a struggle and enthusing the gallery with their desire. When the handlers were set for the break, the judges inquired of their readiness, and hearing the affirmative, authorized the dogs' release.

"Let 'em go, boys."

SIXTEEN

To hear Tom relate what happened next is to hear a voice thrilled by a man's finest dog in its finest hour. The dogs, Bandit to the right and Deputy to the left, bolted from the break sizzling afire. They leapt almost splashless across Timothy Creek at the first turn in the tractor path, the water not dampening their ardor. Past the creek, Bandit kept to the path, which now widened some, while Deputy disappeared into the piney woods. Liam followed to scout and soon called point. Tom and Judge Wilky went to the call. The gallery and Judge Kane continued along behind Buck and Bandit.

Judge Wilky marked the single quail find at five minutes, Deputy steady to wing and shot amid the hawthorn and mulberry under the canopy of Alabama pines. Deputy was then collared and released . . . "hie on." He left the woods and returned to the tractor path now some six furlongs rear of Bandit, ground that he covered quickly, only to come out into the fringe of the sedge fields, where he spied Bandit on point and froze to a halt in honor.

Old Tom says it was the prettiest honor you are ever likely to see (he kicks his good leg forward, thrusts out his arm and commands "*en garde*" as he tells it). Deputy stood statuesque some thirty yards up from Bandit's point, as Buck moved in to flush. Upon the flush, a covey of a half dozen quail burst mottled brown into the air in all directions, Buck making shot. The judges' cards showed the find at twelve minutes, both dogs showing perfect manners before an appreciative gallery, Deputy rightly credited with the honor, or "back," as it is also called.

Released anew, the dogs continued their fevered pace, always to the front, hell bent for leather. Although the flats were open for acres, each dog often would tend toward the likely bird cover of the tree lines and often would be gone from sight there or otherwise would be lost in the tall grasses over the knolls. When a dog was gone from view and seemingly unresponsive to its handler's yodel - a staccato song of "ay-yups" and "aw-rights" meant to keep the dog on course - its scout would be sent to locate. Liam found Deputy on point in a copse of hazel alder, arrow wood and honey locust over a distant rise at twenty minutes; Tall Charlie called point along a Timothy Creek gully at thirty. At this stage of the brace, Deputy's two finds and a back gave him a scorekeeper's edge.

Then it happened. When you hear Old Tom tell of it, the thrill in his voice turns to melancholy.

The trial gait of a Tennessee Walker is just as its name implies, a walk, although at a working pace. The field trial handler will seldom urge his horse beyond a flat walk, but occasionally he may quicken pace in order to quickly reach a dog seen on point at a far-off ride. Rarely, if ever, a handler may bring his horse to a fast walk approaching a canter and then only if authorized by the judges. This day, however, when both dogs were seen careening to an apparent shared point furthermost to the front, Buck looked to Judge Kane, received a nod, and spurred his horse on. Tom obliged his gray gelding to follow. Over the cold, hardened, rutted ground of the tractor path, in the jostle of the canter, Tom's saddle slipped and he tumbled from the horse hard to the ground.

Liam went to Tom quickly, as did the Judge Wilky and members of the gallery; but Tall Charlie rode past with barely a glance, and Buck himself had paid Tom no never mind to begin with. He didn't even glance back over his shoulder when he was passed by Tom's rider less gelding. The overcast day broke into a chilly rain. Tom was sorely injured and taken from the field in the back of a faded and rusty red pick-up truck. His hip broken, he would not soon ride in a major competition again. Later, when Liam examined Tom's saddle, the cinch strap showed an unusual tear, as if it had been sliced by a sharp blade.

Oh…but say…I'm sorry…would you like another glass of chocolate milk?

How about a cookie?

I think that here is as good of a place as any to take another pause, and that perhaps we might leave Tom Quinn for a moment, so that I can tell you about Rooster. Tom's going to be all right, you'll see, and we'll come back to him again in a bit; Tom and Liam, and Amy, too. You'll like Amy.

Oh yeah, and the pooka. I told you there was a pooka, right?

PART TWO

ROOSTER

ONE

Those who venture often in and among the woods and forests know for truth that there are pixies, sprites and faeries.

We didn't know Tom Quinn back in those days. As I told you in the beginning, we didn't meet Tom until much later in his life. How we met him, and the part we play in this story . . . in which you might find a bit of poetic license or fantasy, but which you may take for the truth . . . begins in the picture pages of a coffee-table book, out of which leapt a coarse-haired, orange dog with long floppy ears and yellow eyes, as rare a dog as your whimsy might conjure or imagine.

A good number of months had passed since we had to put down our family dog, a bull terrier named Woodrow, when one evening at dinner time, as I looked out of our kitchen window, I saw his black and white ghost run across our backyard in the shadows of the trees. Turning toward the dinner table, I mentioned to Jan that perhaps it was time for us to get another dog.

"What's wrong with Sparky?" she asked with surprise.

Mike looked up from his meal and put down his fork. "I'd like to get a hunting dog, Dad," he said. "I was looking through this book and saw the neatest dog. It's an Italian dog. They call it a versatile dog because it does a variety of things, like point and retrieve and even swim. Want to see it?" He got up from the table.

"What about Sparky?" Jan repeated in earnest.

Before Mike even returned with the book, I was protesting about the time and trouble involved in owning a dog meant for the outdoors. "They're a lot of work, Mike. You have to exercise them a lot. You're sixteen and will be going to college soon. Who's going to take care of it? Besides, they're meant for the woods and fields and for doing the things nature meant for them to do. It wouldn't be right to get such a dog and then keep it cooped up in the house and yard. You gonna see to that? Besides, you don't like to go bird hunting with me as it is."

"That's because we don't have a huntin' dog, and all we do is walk the fields and seldom get anything . . . unless we go with someone who has a dog. If we had our own dog, and it was a good one, then we could hunt more often," Mike answered as he returned to the table with the book, Sparky waddling behind him, wondering what the commotion was all about. "Here, look at this dog. It's a Spinone. Ain't he neat looking?"

"Let me see," said Jan, taking the book from Mike. "I still don't understand what's wrong with Sparky."

"He doesn't hunt. And, besides, he's your dog," Mike chided.

"No he's not, he's the family dog," Jan admonished sternly.

"If you can call him a dog," Mike snickered light heartedly, as Sparky is his pal.

Sparky's a mop of long, wavy, white-streaked, black hair with legs . . . a Havanese . . . La Chispa Grande . . . The Big Spark . . . a Cuban breed of dog. I was wrong when I said he waddled. He struts a kind of Latin swagger. Does the habanera. Only eleven inches tall, he got up on his hind legs, put his front paws up on Jan's aproned lap, and gave her a look as if to say, "You talking about me? What?" She pet his head as she continued reading.

TWO

It didn't say so much in Mike's book, but Mother Nature did not intend the Spinone for the sport of field trialing. It's a too big, bearded pokiness. If you did find such as it among the cowboys of the old West, as I said you might imagine an English pointer, it would be the chuck wagon cook, the faithful sidekick, the Gabby Hayes. If you imagined it on a chessboard, where the English pointer is a rook, the Spinone would be a pawn, moving just a square at a time, but nevertheless capable of bringing about a mate. It is, after all, a pointing dog, but not cowboy like. It is too much the romantic, more of a poet than a wrangler.

Anyway, field trialing wasn't our interest at the time. Heck, we knew nothing of it. We just read what was said in that coffee table book with a mind toward another dog, one that Mike and I might hunt over, something a bit more than a eleven-inch, Latin floor sweeper, as much as we otherwise cherished The Big Spark. Jan was still petting his head as we read over her shoulder.

"It is adorable looking," she said, "but big. Is it really orange?"

"Orange with yellow eyes," said Mike.

"I don't know, Mike."

"Let's find someone who has one and go see it, Dad."

Which is what we did . . . that and a bit more. We found a breeder not too far away. We called to inquire and learned that his Lucy had recently had a litter. All were gone except one, he said. He invited us to visit. "You'll love the breed," he said. He would guaranty that the dog would hunt. "Great companion," he said. "Real affectionate . . . A lover . . . Yeah, he has an orange coat with yellow eyes," he said.

"All right, how about we come up this Sunday?" I asked.

"Sure."

So we did.

What you might say about a breeder's house is that it is owned by his dogs, leastwise a couple of rooms and a good bit of the furniture. That's who greeted us when we arrived, a Mrs. I presumed, very friendly, as a host should be. From the back of the house we heard, "Come on in, I'll be right with you," accompanied by a clang and jangle of utensils or tools. "Lucy will show you her pup. She's a good dog."

"Where's the pup," I asked our hostess, and Lucy escorted us across a hall to the nursery, but the pup was nowhere to be found. Returning to the foyer, we next followed Lucy out to the backyard, where she stopped sharply, standing like an impatient mother with a hand on her hip. There in the flower garden the pup lay on its back, a ball of orange fur, pawing up at a hovering blue butterfly.

Mike hunched and called, "Here pup . . . here pup." He clapped his hands, "Come on, boy." A little louder, "Here, pup." The butterfly fluttered away. The pup sat up and then pokied over. He sniffed at Mike's offered hand and, finding no treat, lazily returned to his flower bed. At about that time, the breeder, Mr. Mann, came out of the house wearing a carpenter's cover-all, "Hello . . . hello." Lucy went to his side. I turned and introduced myself, shaking hands. Mike did the same.

THREE

"So, I see that you've met Lucy," said Mr. Mann, "and seen the pup. What do you think? Cute little fella, isn't he? He's the last one. We call him 'Squirt,' but, you can call him whatever you want, of course. Here, Squirt. Come on boy. Here, Squirt. Orange with yellow eyes, just like you wanted, right? Here, Squirt come on, pup." He pursed his lips and squeaked a whistle.

The pup just sat among the daisies and yarrow; then he rolled on his back. The blue butterfly returned, lit on a flower, and then again hovered over the orange puppy's head, as if engaging him in conversation.

"Who are they?"

"I don't know."

"They gonna take you?"

"Probably not, I guess maybe not. No one has taken me so far . . . took Polly and Rosco and Mabel and Gus . . . I guess maybe not. Nobody wants a Squirt. Anyway, I like it here in the flowers. Do you think they'll take me? I miss Polly."

"I'll go listen."

Mr. Mann scruffed Lucy's neck, "What's wrong with that pup of yours, girl? Well you know, uh, Ed, right? It's Ed, right? Ed and Mike, right? Well you know, Squirt there was the runt of the litter, the last one, so he's a bit shy; but he'll hunt sure enough. I guarantee he'll hunt. Why, you take him home and he doesn't hunt, well then you just bring him back here to me, guaranteed."

"Look at that butterfly, Dad," Mike gestured with a turn of his head.

"Well, you know, Mr. Mann, we want to make sure we get a sound dog. We wouldn't want to take a puppy home and get all attached and such, and then have to think about returning him because of some problem or other. He does seem to be a bit timid. It would be good if we were to see some energy out of him, some spirit. See him show some behavior like a hunting dog. Some point or something. You know? I don't know. He's kind of . . . uh . . . lackadaisical . . . a little pokey. What do you think, Mike?"

"Did you see that butterfly, Dad? It was blue."

The butterfly fluttered away back toward the pup. I watched it. So did Mike. You can take this for the truth. The butterfly flew over to the pup, lit on its nose, then flit right off and away again across the yard to a daisy bed.

"Tag, you're it."

The pup rolled up off the ground and darted across the yard. Reaching where the butterfly had lit upon a yellow daisy, the dog stopped, craned its neck, crooked its right paw, extended out its stubby tail, and held a puppy point for a second or two just before pouncing. Spreading and shredding daisies and giving chase, it dashed around the yard with evident excitement and zest.

Mike gave me a satisfied smile. I turned to a surprised Mr. Mann.

"I guess he'll be all right. We'll take 'im . . . right, Mike?"

"Sure."

FOUR

"You going with them?"

"I guess so."

"Where to?"

"I don't know."

"I'm coming."

"Hey Dad, look, that blue butterfly flew into the car."

"Roll down the window, and it'll fly out again."

What I said once before about a man and a dog, well, that holds just as true for a boy and a pup, except that there are more licks and hugs. And this pup that we got from Mr. Mann, he was all full of licks just about the whole ride home, except when he was sleeping, which he did on Mike's lap. I don't know who was the more contented, Mike or the puppy. I guess a boy and a pup is a happiness, just as nature must surely have intended.

When we got home, there were Jan and Sparky waiting at the door. Jan went right to the pup, taking him out of Mike's arms and giving him a cuddle. The Big Spark? Well, he said something like, "Hey, what's this all about?" When Jan put the pup on the floor in order to make introductions, La Chispa went into a Cuban Guaracha, if you can liken a tantrum to a Spanish dance… song and dance, really, with his yips and yaps and staccato shrieks of static. He danced himself up onto the couch, where he perched and continued his "inhospitablelities."

The puppy was startled, and it was necessary to tell Sparky to quiet down, which is what I did, whereupon he just skulked off to his bed with a harrumph. Mike picked up the pup, and Jan immediately took him away to cuddle and console. "It's okay," she softly whispered as she nuzzled its brow. She brought the pup into the kitchen and poured him a small bowl of water, which he quickly lapped up. Then he turned to investigate his surroundings, not wandering far from where Mike stood in observation.

"What are we going to call him, Mike?"

"I was thinking of something that fits a hunting dog. I don't know, like Scout or something. Or a cowboy name, you know. I don't know. What do you think?

The pup wondered off, sniffing about the house. He found one of Sparky's abandoned toys and, figuring that a toy is meant to be played with, he pounced on it. Sparky leapt up from his bed and roughly snatched the toy away with a growl. The pup didn't put up any fuss. He just watched as Sparky sauntered off. Then, suddenly, he gave what would have been a howl except for his being just a puppy. It went sort of like "wroooo, wrrroooo, wroooo." Sparky ignored him, but we all couldn't help but to laugh.

"I got it," said Mike excitedly, "you know that John Wayne cowboy, Rooster Cogburn? Let's call the puppy Rooster. That's a great name. Hey, he's a bird dog and his name is Rooster, get it? Wroooster. Hey Rooster, come here boy. Come on." And, he went and picked up the little dog. "Wrooo . . . Rooster. That's your name boy. What d'ya think, huh? Rooster." He scruffed its forehead and tickled its ear, "Good boy."

Sparky sat over in the corner, chawing on that toy of his like it was the stub of a Cuban cigar.

FIVE

"Hey, Dad, remember that blue butterfly?"

Jan was curious, "What butterfly?"

I began to explain, putting aside a magazine. "When we were at Mr. Mann's …" But, Mike was continuing.

"I saw another one just like it. It was like it was following me and Rooster along on our walk. Funniest thing . . ."

"What blue butterfly?" Jan persisted.

". . .it would flit back at Roo then zip off and Roo would pull on the leash to chase it, just like at Mr. Mann's . . . like he has this thing for blue butterflies."

"You know buddy that dog is now getting to the age where you have got to start giving him some training, if you're going to hunt with him in the fall. Pointing butterflies and pointing birds are two different things. How old is he now? What, ten, eleven months?"

"He's going on more than a year and a half," said Jan. "I've never heard of a blue butterfly before."

"Neither had I," said Mike, "Strangest thing. I'm sure that it can't be the same butterfly 'cause butterflies don't live all that long…strangest thing, though, huh?

"Maybe it's a pooka," I suggested.

"A what?" Mike and Jan quizzed in unison.

"Just some old Irish fancy…never mind," I shook my head and picked up the magazine.

You're right, Dad. I think that I'll take Roo over to the Crooked Branch Management area on Saturday and let him run. I don't expect that there'll be any birds there at this time of year, but I'll bet that he'd like being off the leash and just running."

"You best keep him on a long lead, if you're going to run him, Mike."

"Oh, he won't run off, Dad. He stays close. He'll come when called. I'll watch him. Want to come?"

"I can't this Saturday."

Jan wandered over to the kitchen window. "Where's Sparky?"

"He and Rooster are out back chasing each other around."

Roo was now better than three times Sparky's size, and you'd think that his gangly legs would give him the race, but Sparky was quick and spry enough, and just sage enough to put a tag on the slower, orange galoot. Like a bushwhacker, he'd wait in ambush for Rooster to make a wrong turn, and then he'd pounce. And, yapping . . . gee whiz that Sparky could yip and yap and growl. You'd think Rooster would let himself be tagged just to quiet the confounded yapping. They'd become good pals, though, as odd a pair as they might seem to most eyes. It is a funny thing, what fancy nature can work. And, in that work there plays a blue butterfly.

"Where're you goin'?" The butterfly asked Rooster.

"Mike's taking me somewhere to run."

"Without a leash?"

"Some wildlife place, he says."

"There'll be spring blooms?"

"I guess so."

"I'm coming." The butterfly nestled in hiding beneath a floppy, orange ear and fell asleep.

So fancy that, a boy, an orange dog and a sprite of a blue butterfly. As it's often said, there are more wonders in nature than of what the books do tell. Tom Quinn knew as much, and he kept an Irish faith in the fanciful despite a few bumps, rough tumbles and hard knocks along life's way.

Which, I guess, brings us back to Tom.

SIX

After Tom and Liam returned home from Alabama, Tom was put to convalescing with his fractured hip. There was little he could do by way of running and training dogs, and his misery was all the greater for it. Liam took many of the responsibilities on himself, but he didn't have Tom's enthusiasm. In part, I suppose, because Liam didn't much take to English pointers, they being somewhat too high strung for his liking. Liam preferred the English setter.

There isn't much that's cowboy-like in an English Setter. Unclipped, it has a long, flowing coat and feathered tail and looks more suited for the show ring than for sport. Clipped, it might call to mind sun-bleached, ticked, and fringed buckskin, if there needs to be a western conceit. There is a grace to its run, windswept and ephemeral, but rugged nonetheless, like a bareback rider of the plains. The setter's point is regal in aspect, commanding, not threatening like a gun slinger. If it is to be compared to a chess piece like the others in our story, then it might be thought of as the queen.

Preferences aside, Liam took his responsibilities to heart, even handling Tom's pointers in field trials for several seasons. Soon, though, Liam acquired a setter to his liking and then shortly another. Before long, Tom's kennel had a string of both breeds, which the brothers campaigned along the East Coast. One setter in particular, Star Chief, garnered multiple titles and almost stole Tom's affections. But, there just wasn't enough time for a setter to completely win Tom over, as before long, age and the painful remnants of his injury kept him from staying long in the competition saddle, and his campaigning came to a halt.

Unable to compete, Tom took solely to breeding and training, mostly for other handlers. His dogs had good lineage, especially the Deputy line. Even Star Chief's get were highly sought after. A field trialer could be confident in the quality of his entry if his dog was Tom Quinn bred and trained. Leastwise, the handler wouldn't be embarrassed by the dog. Tom's reputation grew.

The success of Tom's kennel enabled him to bring on help as needed, which became more and more the case, since Tom could spend less and less time in the saddle and the arthritis hobbled his walk. The training was mainly done at Tom's small farm in western Massachusetts. Several times a week, though, the dogs would be crated, the horses trailered, and Tom and crew would go train the dogs on pen-raised quail and captured pigeons at the Crooked Branch Wildlife Management Area, a rolling land of knee-high field grasses edged by woodlands of black oak and red maple and evergreens, with islands of hazel alder, white paper birch, and blue cedar.

It was at Crooked Branch that Mike first met them . . . Tom and Liam and Tom's niece, Amy and Tom's wife, Helen . . . on that day when Mike first took Rooster out for a run off-leash. It was an early April afternoon, chilly enough for jackets, but with a bright sunlight that played amidst the still-bare woods and winter-thinned fields, inviting spring forget-me-nots and miter-wort to bloom.

SEVEN

As Mike drove into Crooked Branch looking for a place to let Rooster run, he came upon Tom's set-up, the red flannel shirted old man sitting hunched on the tailgate of an old, gray pick-up truck, his wife Helen in the cab, the truck and horse trailer beside a string of pointers and setters . . . some animated, some at rest, some sitting stoically with a forward gaze . . . and off a short distance, two riders returning behind a pointer restrained on a long gray lead.

Mike was curious and drove up to learn of their activity. Tom gave the approaching tan Jeep a quick glance but returned to observing the riders, as if an unknown visitor was of no particular interest to him. Mike's an amiable enough kid, and he wasn't timid in making an introduction.

He parked and got out the Jeep, then approached the old man, "Hi . . . I'm Mike."

"Hello, Mike."

Mike extended a hand that Tom grasped warmly enough, although Tom never took his eyes from the returning riders. Mike turned to watch and stood quietly. Amy arrived first with the pointer, dismounted and returned the dog to its place on the string with the others, then gave it some water from a white, three-gallon container with a hand-pumped spray hose, squirting the water into the panting dog's eager mouth, which spilled more than it swallowed. She made an inquisitive, passing glance at Mike, as he appeared to be about her age, and then looked back to her dog. Liam rode directly to Tom.

"He did pretty good," Liam reported as he dismounted. "Crept a bit on that quail in the yarrow, but he steadied for the shot . . . ran real nice overall."

"The owner doesn't want any creeping, Liam. Didn't find that other bird you planted neither, now did he? Or the several others we've flushed since earlier?" Tom remarked. "He should have, in this bit of breeze."

"Well, yeah, but who knows. What do you think, Amy?"

Amy walked over to the truck, again shooting a fleeting, inquisitive glance at Mike as she passed. "Well, if that bird is still out there, then Queen will find it when we run her, and likely the others, too. Queeny's nose won't miss a bird in the field with this breeze." Amy replied.

"Plant another couple o' quail for her anyhow, Amy. We need to get her to steady-up better on what she does find." Tom turned to Mike as Amy went over to fetch the birds.

"Well, Mike, what can we do for you?" Turning over his shoulder, he yelled towards the cab of the truck, "Helen . . . this here is Mike," Helen smiled and nodded from behind the windshield.

"Are you guys dog trainers?"

"We're a kennel. We train dogs."

"Pretty neat . . . with horses and all? I've just got a dog for bird hunting that I brought up here to run a bit, except, I don't know much about what I'm doing' . . . training a dog and all. It's my first hunting dog. Mind if I watch? Maybe I can learn somethin?"

"You're welcome to watch. What kinda dog do you have, Mike?"

"Well, he's just a young one, little over a year. Can I bring him out to watch?"

"Just so long as he's leashed, I don't want him bothering' my dogs."

Mike went to the Jeep to get Rooster. Amy cast a mystified glance toward Liam, then she went and stood by Tom and watched the boy with particular curiosity, forgetting about the quail that she held loosely in her hand.

EIGHT

Mercury's wings are on his heels. The wings of Canis are on his heart.

Now, if Tom was worried that his dogs might be bothered were Rooster not leashed, well, he hadn't anticipated the mere aspect of the orange dog. There was commotion sure enough, although I'd guess that the correct word is hilarity. The gangly, orange coated, yellow-eyed, floppy-eared pokiness was not what anyone had expected…dogs or people.

The excitement among the other dogs was evident in their agitation. Should you not be inclined to believe that dogs have a sense of humor, well then, you would otherwise have to explain those on Tom's string that were on their backs pawing at the sky. Among the humans, Tom crinkled his face with a smile, as did Helen, while neither Liam nor Amy could contain their amusement.

"What the heck is that?" Liam crowed half bent over the fender of the truck. Amy, struck with surprise, accidentally let loose the quail she had held and it flew off, causing the dogs' further excitement as they barked and pulled at their chains in an effort to give chase. The loss of the quail irked Tom, but the contagion of Liam's laughter and Amy's merriment tempered his irritation. He contained his own laughter, giving a quick look back at Helen, who erased her smile and shook her head with motherly-like disapproval.

"Well, well, Mike, what kind of dog is that?" Tom asked.

"This is Rooster. He's a Spinone."

"And he hunts?" Liam hawed in disbelief. Amy smiled, but nervously looked away as she did, loosely covering her smile with her gloved hand that didn't hide the sparkle of her eyes.

"Well yeah, he's supposed to. I haven't been hunting with him yet. But, he's supposed to hunt. He has a natural point; at least I've seen him point." Mike was a bit taken aback by their reactions but not humbled. He even smiled a bit himself. He looked over to Amy, hoping to find some evidence that someone his own age did not think him a complete fool. She just looked to the ground with a shy smile that slightly dimpled her flushed cheek.

"If he ain't been hunting, then what'd you see him point?" Liam challenged, lightly elbowing Amy in the ribs. Again, she turned away to hide her smile, brushing her auburn hair away from her green eyes.

Despite spending his life among pointers and setters, Tom was nonetheless what you might call a 'man-of-all-dogs,' having a genuine affection for the four-legged critters overall. Seeing that Mike was becoming somewhat embarrassed, he quieted things down with a wave. He slowly let himself down from the tailgate and with a limp approached Rooster and extended his hand, intent on giving Roo a pat on the head. Instead, Rooster rolled over on his back and begged a rub of his belly. Tom obliged. "Friendly fella, huh?" scratching Roo's belly, "That's a good boy."

Tom straightened and turned to Mike, "Well, Mike, you seem like a good kid. I don't know about that mongrel dog of yours; but I'll tell you what, why don't we see what he's got? We're going to run Queen next, but you go and put your dog on that string with the other dogs there, and we'll let you both watch. Then we'll see what your Rooster does. How's that sound?"

"Sure, thanks. That's great." Mike replied with a grateful smile and again looked over to Amy, hoping to find some encouragement. But, she just blushed a bit and looked away, first to Liam, then to the ground, then over to the string of dogs so as to direct Mike's attention to the opportunity Tom had offered, her eyes suggesting that he was right to accept.

Mike returned a bashful smile of uncertain comprehension, adjusted the Red Sox cap on his head, and led a somewhat reluctant Rooster over to the string where he found a free link of chain at one end, to the right of a young, tri-color setter female, and attached the chain to Roo's collar, patting him on the head. "You stay here, Roo. . .we'll watch, and then they said they'll take you for a run with some birds. You haven't seen birds yet. You just have to find them and point 'em and show these folks that you're a hunting' dog, cause that's what you are, see. You stay here." He patted Roo's head . . . "Good boy."

Rooster sat quietly as Mike returned to stand near Tom by the truck. Liam, still grinning, stood hunched over, hands on his knees, slowly shaking his head, wondering at Tom's intentions. Amy rode off to plant the quail. The little tri-colored setter turned towards Rooster.

NINE

"I'm Pokey," the little setter offered amiably.

"Me, too," Rooster bashfully replied.

"No, I mean that's my name. It's short for Pocahontas…Star Chief's Pocahontas…that's my name. Star Chief's my dad. Queen's my mom. That's Queen there with Liam. She's going out now. What's your name?"

"Oh, I'm Roo."

"Roo what? Don't you have more of a name than that? Who's your dad?"

"My full name is Rooster…just Rooster."

"That's just silly. A rooster is a bird. We've got a rooster at home…a silly one, too…wakes everyone up all the time…crowing and such."

"Well I'm not a bird, of course, and most times Sparky wakes me up."

"Who's Sparky? My dad was a champion. My mom's going to be a champion, too. Me too, someday…Mr. Quinn says so. Is Sparky a rooster?"

"No, Sparky is a dog. He's my pal. But he doesn't sleep late like I do. What's a champion?"

"A field trial champion…That's what we do. We run in field trials. We're here training with Mr. Quinn. That's Mr. Quinn there sitting on the truck. Mr. Quinn is the best. I'm going to be a champion when he finishes training me."

"Me too."

"You can't be a champion."

"Why not?"

"Because, you don't look like a champion, at least I've never seen any champion that looked like you. I mean, you're kind of cute with your floppy ears and yellow eyes but where's your muscles? You've got to have muscles to be a champion . . . and heart."

"Where do I get muscles?"

"You're silly. Look, watch my mom run. You'll see. To be a champion you've got to be strong and fast and have lots of desire. That's what I've got . . . lots of desire. Lots of heart, that's what Mr. Quinn says. That's why I'm going to be a champion, wings on my heart."

Rooster turned to watch Queen run just as Liam released her. She broke fast and straight, then veered left towards a tree line, only to cut back into the breeze. She was strong, she was fast, and she showed lots of desire, all as Tom explained to Mike.

"That's a good dog there, Mike. See how she takes to the task? Now, we don't expect as much from that, that ah. . .what kind of dog did you say you got?"

"A Spinone."

"Well now, you see, that's a mongrel breed, Mike. We wouldn't expect such performance from a dog like that. I'm sure he's a good dog, Mike. Just, he ain't a dog like Queen there, nor like these pointers and setters we got. See? But. . .Oh there. . .see now, Queen has gone on point. Watch this."

Meanwhile, a black ticked pointer chained to the left of the little setter rose up off his hunches, tautly flexed, yawned and turned to her. "What are you talking to him for? He ain't our kind." He snarled with an eye slanted towards Rooster.

TEN

The little setter told the pointer, "Hush!" She turned towards Rooster. "Don't mind him. That's Chet, which is short for Winchester… Deputy's Winchester. He thinks he's a big shot." She giggled at her pun.

Rooster had not heard Chet snarl. He was rapt in Queen's performance and, without turning to acknowledge the little setter, he softly muttered, "Uh huh."

Queen was as still as a picture as she made point. She held regally proud through the flush and shot. Upon being released, she sped on to the hunt and continued enthusiastically until coming upon the second bird that Amy had hidden. Again her point was worth beholding, her tail firm at noon, its feathery hairs slightly whisked by the breeze. She hunted anew after this second find, but when after a good while she went without further bird work, she was leashed and returned.

"You see?" asked Tom, "like an oil painting, huh?" "A setter on point is perhaps the most often painted of all game dogs. Beautiful, isn't she?" Mike silently nodded.

Tom continued, "Well, after Liam puts Queen back on the string, I'll have him plant a bird for your dog. Can you ride a horse? You can go out with Amy, and we'll see what that dog of yours does. You just let Amy work him. You can ride, right?

"I've been trail riding," Mike answered. "I guess I can ride well enough for what I've seen Amy do. I'd like that pretty much, thanks Mr. Quinn. Should I go get Rooster?"

"These are Tennessee Walking Horses, Mike, so you should be alright. I don't expect that dog of yours will give you any reason to gallop for gosh sakes. Just let Amy handle your dog. Do you have a long lead to bring him out on?" As Liam returned to the truck, Tom turned to him. "Liam, get a long lead for Mike's dog. Amy, you handle Mike's dog … show 'im a bird before he goes out. Mike, this here is Amy."

"Hi."

"Liam, you plant a quail for that dog. Hey, Liam, Queen never did find any leftover quail, did she?" Liam shook his head.

Amy answered, "I'm surprised, because she usually finds everything… must really have flown off somewhere. Queen covered most of the field. I don't know."

Liam grinned and gave Amy a soft elbow to the ribs, "Maybe that mongrel will find them," and they both snickered as they went about their separate chores.

Amy grabbed a quail from the bird box and then walked with Mike over to Rooster. Holding the squawking quail by its legs, its wings frantically flapping, she presented it before Rooster, who seemed to have no interest, while the other dogs on the string rose up and barked and yelped in excitement. Amy, shrugging her shoulders at Roo's disinterest, turned and looked at Tom quizzically, while Tom, chagrined, shook his head slowly. Mike urged Rooster to no avail.

Handing the long, coiled, orange lead to Mike, Liam said, "Well, just take him up to the line on this here lead, and we'll see if he's more interested when he encounters a bird in the field."

Mike attached the lead to Roo's collar and removed him from the string. "Come on Rooster," he said, "Come on, you've got to have desire, if you want to be a hunting dog. I know ya can do it. Come on, boy." Rooster went hesitantly along as if he were a child being brought for a visit to a barber.

Chet turned to Pokey, "You see that? Did you see that? What kind of dog is that anyhow? Not our kind, like I said." He turned to the pointer on his left, "Did you see that?" Pokey looked at him disapprovingly and quickly turned away shaking her head. She was unwilling to join in their mockery, and she was more than slightly curious as to how Rooster would perform once he was loose in the field.

When they reached the line, Mike handed the lead to Liam, who set up Rooster for a release. After fumbling a bit with the stirrup, Mike mounted Liam's bay gelding and wiggled himself into the saddle. Amy waited astride her mare. She brushed the hair away from her eyes, pulled down on her cap and looked across the way to Tom, who gave a slight shrug of doubt with his shoulders. When Mike announced that he was ready, Liam unleashed Rooster and sharply and loudly commanded the dog, "*Hie on!*" with a slap to the back of Rooster's head.

ELEVEN

Now, something must've spooked Rooster. Maybe it was Liam's loud command, or maybe it was the idea of having a couple of horses snorting down his back, but something got him running faster than Mike had ever seen before and surely faster than anyone else had expected. Of course, a Spinone doesn't run with the speed and energy of a pointer, not "hell bent for leather," like I told you earlier. Nope, it galumphs, more like long, leaping strides, like a series of bounding broad jumps, two legs at a time, like a big, floppy eared, scared jack rabbit.

It was a sight … even caused Helen to clap giddily from her seat in the cab of the truck. Amy smiled over at Mike, whose mouth was wide open in surprise. Tom slapped his knee with a hoot, and then cringed at the pain. Even the other dogs on the string stood up, appearing to take notice, especially the little setter. Liam just stood gawking with his hands on his hips.

Rooster's run took him out quite a ways before he slowed and began to meander about in the tall, early spring grasses, often lost from sight. As Amy and Mike would get closer, he would just take-off anew. Galumph, galumph, and galumph, running mostly straight with no obvious purpose other than to get away. He was running against the wind, his droopy ears pinned back like the wings on Mercury's silver sandals, and then he suddenly stopped and reversed his course. He seemed curious about an area clustered with some meadow-rue and ragwort. Apparently there was something that he wanted to investigate.

He circled around, his nose held high, inhaling, searching the breeze. He began to creep slowly, stalking. Then he stopped stone still, except for his tail, which wagged excitedly. Flagging, it's called in the sport. Not a good thing for a pointing dog, whose point is supposed to be staunchly intent and convincing, but the fact that Rooster stopped meant that Amy should dismount and do some investigating herself, although she questioned whether Rooster was actually pointing a bird.

She approached Rooster cautiously, softly "whoaing" him, though Roo had not yet learned that command. Roo turned to watch Amy's approach. Then, he craned his neck further back over his shoulder to look towards Mike for some assurance or comfort as Amy slowly moved in front of him.

Now, a quail, being a small bird, is not often easily seen by the handler, like a pheasant might be seen. And unlike the pheasant, the quail doesn't usually run. Instead, the quail will burrow into the grasses to hide itself, so that the handler has to kick around in the grasses with her boots in order to flush the bird, which is what Amy did. All the while Rooster stood steady, his tail now still, his point more convincing and directing Amy's search, Amy looking back to him for assurances. "Where is it boy? Is there a bird here? Show me."

Suddenly the bird flushed. Rooster stood and watched. Amy looked at Mike, and they both smiled. Amy walked back towards Rooster, intending to place him on a lead, and as she did, she drew her blank gun and fired. Rooster held his stance, but the crack of the gun awoke the stowaway butterfly. "Miterwort!" the butterfly exclaimed excitedly, and she zipped off from under Rooster's ear, unseen by either Mike or Amy, but not missed by Rooster, who suddenly dashed off with the same speed at which he had begun his run, if not even a bit faster.

Amy turned and looked to Mike with surprise. She hurriedly mounted her horse, and they followed Roo, their own pace now a bit quicker than their earlier walk, which caused Mike to bounce around in his saddle as if he were seated on a spring. They lost Rooster as he crested a knoll and headed toward the far, shadow gray tree line of the horizon.

TWELVE

Rooster yelled after the fleeing butterfly, "Hey, where're you going?" But, all that the wind carried back to him in reply was "*Miterwoooort!*"

The miterwort, with its tiny, fringed white flowers, is a fragile, April woodlands bloom. The blue butterfly's objective was the gray, leafless woodland bordering the sallow Crooked Branch fields, a good distance from Rooster's first point. Following the butterfly, Rooster crested a knoll, vanished from sight, and bounded across a brook with an unheard splash.

Upon reaching the height of the knoll, Amy and Mike again caught sight of the dog. "Where's he goin?" Amy asked, although mostly to herself. "Don't know," Mike answered. "Should I call him?" "No…no, let's see what he's up to." They quickened their pace. Mike, jostled all the more by the quicker gait, held tight to the saddle horn, a bit unsure of himself and fearing that his horse might run away with him. Rooster entered the woods, and he was again lost from sight.

"Where are you going?" Rooster called again to the butterfly, but this time there was no reply. "Where are you?" Again, there was no reply. Rooster slowed to a walk. He looked to his left and then to his right. He chose a course unimpeded by undergrowth and dashed off weaving among the standing trees and leaping the fallen, pushing through the laurel and scrub. "Where are you?" he called, and again there was no reply. So he ran on, his direction dictated by the paths of least obstruction. Then he heard a garbled, "Over here," as from a mouth busy chewing.

He slowed, turned and ambled in the direction of the voice, finding the blue butterfly lit upon the miterwort. He was about to chide the sprite for leading him on a tiring chase, when something in the woody air commanded his attention. He sniffed and then inhaled deeply. He circled as if plotting a perimeter, the circle getting smaller, like the eddy of tub water flowing down a drain, until he came to a rigidly stout stance, his tail extended taut and unflagging, a small covey of quail milling in the bush before him, five in all.

Amy and Mike had hobbled their horses and entered the woods on foot. They made their way apart, although within a soft shout of each other, seeking the runaway dog, at times calling out for him.

"Rooster," called Mike.

"Hey dog," hollered Amy, "where are you?"

Then, Mike saw him. "Look," he beckoned to Amy.

"Easy, Mike." Amy cautioned, "Your dog's on point. I couldn't tell for sure the first time, but there's no question about it now. Wait. Let me approach him." Amy cautiously moved toward Rooster, who stood firm but for a quick glance over his shoulder at the intruder.

As she neared the dog, Amy could see the quail milling about, and she knew that they could see and hear her too. She quickly moved ahead of the dog and noisily swept her foot across the ground to startle the quail to flight. The birds burst mottled brown into the air in all directions. Amy drew and fired her blank gun. Rooster held steady and allowed himself to be collared away, choosing not, or perhaps being just too tired, to renew his chase of the troublesome butterfly, which he watched fly off with the shot, trailing the quail as if a tardy member of their covey, out above the still bare tree tops, into a graying April sky.

Mike felt a sense of both wonder and confusion. He wondered at his dog's drive. What could have impelled Rooster to charge off and rush far off into the woods like he did? And, he was confused about his feelings towards this girl he had only just met, but who had taken him on horseback across newly awakened spring fields to chase a seemingly wayward dog that was losing itself in the shadows of the still winter grey woods. And, she knew what she might find there, and she knew how to find it. Was he lost now, himself? She was leading his dog on a long rope from aback her horse, and he was following her. How far, he wondered. Amy looked back over her shoulder and smiled.

THIRTEEN

"You should've seen it, Dad." Mike was beaming excitedly while telling us about his day at Crooked Branch with Tom Quinn. He tossed his cap on the couch and began removing his cotton jacket.

Rooster, however, was splayed out in a corner of the den, achingly exhausted. Sparky tried to get him to play. "Hey, what's the matter with you?" He grabbed a toy, and teasingly shook it in Rooster's face, "You want this, hey? Come and get it." He ran off to the other end of the room, abruptly made an about face, grinning teasingly, his tail wagging, "Hey, what's the matter with you?" But, Rooster just covered his head with his fore paws and groaned, "Oooooooooh."

"It was really something," Mike continued. "At first they all laughed at Rooster, and said he was a mongrel and stuff, and then he showed 'em. He showed them good, alright. He found all the birds, even the ones that Queen didn't find, at least that's what Amy told Mr. Quinn." Mike was pacing back and forth.

"Who's Queen?" Jan interrupted.

"She's one of Mr. Quinn's dogs. He's got a whole string of dogs, pointers and setters that he trains, and Queen's a setter. There's also Chet, and Pokey...I think Pokey likes Rooster...and there's Biscuit, and some others; but Queen is a field trial winner, and she's supposed to have this great nose, see, but Rooster was the one that found the birds. He found five of 'em...a covey it's called, or a bevy...in the woods. You could hardly see them among the brown fallen leaves and sticks and shrubs of the forest floor. Then they burst up into the air when Amy flushed with her boot. It was real neat.

Mr. Quinn says Rooster has got a good nose, and Liam and Amy agreed. Amy said he really does and Liam just stood there nodding his head in agreement. Mr. Quinn says that Roo could be a good trial dog, except he doesn't have much stamina, and he runs kind of funny, Mr. Quinn said." Mike threw his coat on the couch and walked towards the kitchen.

"Who's this Pokey dog?" Jan asked, curious at the suggestion of some girlish flirtations with 'her' Rooster. She followed Mike into the kitchen, but looked back at Rooster, splayed on the floor.

"Well, she's a little setter that was on the string next to Roo," replied Mike, reaching into the fridge for a soda. "When we brought Roo back from his run, he was all exhausted and panting and all hang-dog like, and this little setter, Pokey, leapt at him playfully, licking at him and stuff, although Rooster was so tired, he just collapsed as we chained him up. He barely took water when Amy tried to give it to him. He just collapsed right there, panting away. He was real beat. He must've run several miles, I bet. I was glad I had a horse."

"What horse?" Jan asked with agitated concern. "Did you have a helmet? Where'd you get a horse from anyway? Did you know about this, Ed?" She turned to me somewhat startled.

"No," I answered, as Mike continued.

"It's okay, Ma. It's no big deal. They're just these walking horses. They don't gallop or anything. That's how you train dogs for field trials. It's no big deal." Mike drank thirstily from the soda can.

"Well, what about this Pokey dog?" Jan pried for further gossip.

"Oh, I don't know about that. I'm just saying that it's like everyone was making fun of Rooster at first, and then they all liked him. Except that Chet dog, who kind of looked meanly and snarled at him when we got back. So, I just thought that Pokey at least looked like she was friendly in comparison, that's all. It's nothing." Mike looked into the can of soda then lightly swirled the contents before taking another drink.

Unable to get Rooster to play, Sparky was dancing around our feet, enviously seeking some attention. When he overheard the talk about Pokey and Rooster, he just couldn't let that go. He teased Rooster, "So, you got a girlfriend, huh? He pranced over and planted a loud and exaggerated "smooooooch" in Roo's ear. Rooster just rolled over and moaned some more, "Oooooooooooh."

"Mr. Quinn says that I can bring Roo to train with him and Liam and Amy if I want. And, so long as I help out with the other dogs and stuff, he won't charge me. Can I do it?" Mike directed his question to both Jan and me.

"I suppose so," I answered.

But Jan wasn't too sure. She insisted, "I want you to go with him, Ed, and see what this is all about. Who are these people, anyway? And I don't know about this horse business, either. I don't like any other dog snarling at Rooster, either. Rooster is not the kind of dog to get into fights with other dogs. Even Sparky beats him up. I want you to go with Mike next time to see what this is all about, okay?" She went over to Rooster, stooped and stroked his back. "You're a good boy," she said, "Good boy."

"What do you say, Dad?"

"And, who's that Amy girl?" Jan stood, turned towards Mike and pressed her motherly inquisition. She then looked to me with a command to take point and report.

FOURTEEN

I pretty much understand what Sparky has said about pointing dog dharma and things, but I don't think that it helps to explain all of what happened with Rooster that first day that Mike met Tom Quinn at Crooked Branch. I mean, it does seem as though Rooster did at least find and point that first quail among the meadow-rue and ragwort. So, I guess that it is fair to say that pointing game birds is Rooster's dharma.

But, Amy expressed doubt about Rooster's first point, suggesting that the point was not all that staunch, that it didn't have that "ribs protruding" and "flesh pulsating" intensity that Sparky said that it should have. And, I'm sure that his tail flagged, too. So, it appears that Rooster has a chink in his dharma. Okay, that's a poor pun, I'm sorry, it just came out.

And, what about that blue butterfly; it intervened in Rooster's run now, didn't' it? We can't really say that Rooster actually ran off and found those quail that Queen had supposedly missed all by himself, now can we? I don't think so. Still, I wouldn't disabuse Mike of the idea; he was so excited when he came home.

But, how do we account for that butterfly... as a pooka, a pixie, or a fancy? Is there room in dog dharma for fanciful creatures to lend a hand, to involve themselves, or to play a part in a dog's life every once in a while? Or, is the fanciful world of dogs and butterflies, of sprites and faeries but one single cosmology, so that there really is no intervention, but just the simple unified force of a singular spirituality, a kind of universal, living things oneness, even if some of those things dwell only in our imagination?

Anyway, I'm not sure that I am qualified to explain much about dogs, especially pointing dogs, of which I am still learning, never mind my trying to explain anything to you about pookas, faeries and other such fanciful notions, as they are surely beyond my schooling. It's like Amy tells Mike later on at the barn, you have to believe, and if you believe, then your beliefs become a part of your reality, fanciful as that may be.

I do think, however, that I have somewhat of a better handle on the karma that Sparky spoke about. And, I do think that when Rooster stood steady after Amy's flush of the covey in the woodlot, and then allowed himself to be collared and led away, I do think that was something of Rooster's karma.

Except that, I am just not so sure that Rooster was acting in his own interests, the way that Pete did when he allowed Tom to collar him after he ran off in that North Dakota prairie those many years ago. I don't think that Rooster was looking for companionship with Amy precisely, at least not the way that Pete had sought companionship with Tom, anyhow.

Knowing what I know today, I am kind of inclined to think that Rooster was maybe intervening in Mike's fate, the way that the butterfly had intervened in his. You know, playing a role. Dogs can do that. They can insinuate themselves into your life and then suddenly they bring about a change. They can be a cause and effect. This can be especially true when it comes to companionship between a boy and a girl. Interject a puppy and see what happens. Karma, like Sparky said.

So, maybe there is more to life than the many differences by which we ordinarily define life forces such as boys and dogs and butterflies. Maybe there is running through all of them a singular animation that every once in a while allows them to become one. I'm pretty sure that dogs don't just inhabit the material world by which we define them. Dogs are more than just animated stuff, even if they can be fluffy and cuddlesome like a doll.

A boy and a dog and a boy and a girl and, well, okay, and a sprite of a blue butterfly, they are the fanciful oneness of this tale, them and Sparky and Tom. But, like the chink in Roo's dharma, there's a wrinkle in the fabric of our story, a disturbance in the force, as they say in the movies. Our fable is not all fun and fancy. There is mischief afoot, both two and four.

FIFTEEN

I did go to Crooked Branch as Jan commanded, and I met Tom Quinn, who told me his story as we sat on the tailgate of his pick-up truck and watched his dogs run, just the same as I have told his story to you. And, he told me about how he and Liam did meet up again with Buck Arness and Tall Charlie Hinkle a time or two after Tom's fall at the Alabama Invitational, and how their dogs never were braced again except once, when Liam pulled his dog rather than run with Buck's dog.

It was Buck's dog that bothered Liam, said Tom, although Liam had no liking for the two men either. Tom says that sometimes a dog can have a personality like its owner. You know? Somewhat like how people are often said to look like their dogs. Well, Tom said that Buck's dogs have a reputation for not being mannerly in the field and for causing trouble and such. They're ornery dogs, like their owner, he said. Liam would just as soon not put one of his dogs at risk, Tom said, except maybe if a championship was on the line, which wasn't the case the last time they met.

"They're still around," Tom said, "but we haven't seen them much...they being out in Missouri. Another trainer that I know did run into 'em a couple of years ago at a pheasant futurity in New York, so I guess they may come East now and then. The trainer only knew of them by reputation, and he said the reputation appeared well-earned. He said their pup got disqualified for snarling at its brace mate. Dogs can be like kids. You know...like the acorns that don't fall far from the tree, I guess."

You can kind of understand Tom's meaning, although I can't figure out if either Sparky or Rooster is much like me, or even like Mike or Jan...that Sparky, he's a character. I brought him with me that day I first met Tom, just to take him along for the ride. I let him out of the car, thinking he'd just wander about nearby and enjoy the fresh spring air of early May, the new grasses rising, the trees beginning to leaf.

Well, he promptly assumed this pompous strut, kind of like an army general, chest out and chin high. He marched before Tom's string of pointers and setters as though they were buck privates on parade, each of whom gave him a puzzled look as if to challenge his conceit. Then, Chet said something like, "What do you want, pipsqueak?"

Now, you don't call the Big Spark a "pipsqueak." He may be small, but he's got what they call a Napoleonic complex. He turned on Chet and gave him the old, "You talking to me?" routine, with all kind of yips and yaps and even a bared tooth growl or two thrown in for good measure. Chet wasn't about to back down, but his being chained on the string prevented him from actually assaulting the little Havanese. He reared up on his hind legs, though, growling and pawing the air, so I thought it obligatory that I should intervene, notwithstanding that Tom and Liam got a good laugh out of the fracas.

I put a leash on Sparky and started to lead him back to the car, when again he stopped, this time in front of that little setter, Pokey. He ogled her up and down, took in a few whiffs as dogs are wont to do and then said something to her teasingly.

"You like my buddy, Rooster, huh, Poquita?"

She blushed and turned away.

"Oooh, you do, huh. That's okay, I won't tell anyone."

He sniffed at her some more and then looked over at Rooster with a sly wink and approving nod, in the manner that the French call *entre nous*. I yanked on his leash, sternly commanding him to heal and then walked him back to the car. He stood on the front passenger seat, his paws on the dash, and peered out with a perceptible grin, as though master of all he surveyed. I returned to Tom to apologize.

Tom dismissed my apology. "Nothing of it, Ed, the little dog's got some fight in him, huh?"

"You ought to take him bear hunting," Liam laughed and Amy smiled a dimpled smile that she carried across her shoulder to Mike. Mike returned the smile and then he lowered and slowly shook his head so as to disassociate himself from his relations. He looked to busy himself, but finding nothing, he stood head down with his hands in his pockets, averting the study of her glance.

I spent the day with them and watched them train their dogs, and Rooster, too. Tom had a liking for both Mike and Roo, which was good to see.

"Well, Ed, that dog's a mongrel breed, you know," he said and then repeated what he had told Mike when they first met, "but I give him one thing, he's got a good nose, and he's good mannered. So, he's a pleasure to work with. And your boy's a good kid. It's a pleasure having them both here. We'll see if we can't make a field trialer out of one of 'em." He smiled and there was a twinkle of anticipation in his eyes.

"I appreciate that, Tom," I told him. We shook hands, and I took my leave, turning first to Mike.

"Mike, you mind your manners and you work hard with Mr. Quinn."

"So, I can stay and train then, Dad?" He looked from me to Amy, but she demurely turned away.

"Sure. Who knows, maybe someday you might run Rooster in a field trial," I answered, pushing a jab of jest to tickle his rib. There was something afloat between him and Amy that suggested that Mike was interested in more than just field trials. I would have some explaining to do to Jan when I got home.

SIXTEEN

What Tom told me that day about Buck Arness and Tall Charlie Hinkle wasn't just rumor. Those two never seemed to be happy with the success that they won honestly and they always tried to take by hook or by crook, as it is said. There are the tricks of the trade, of course, and that's one thing, I suppose, but Buck and Tall Charlie, they marked the cards whenever they could. I earlier said of Buck that he had a wolf in his stomach. Charlie was devilish just for the sake of it, that and because of his crony fealty to Buck. He was wiry in stature and wily in demeanor.

Tall Charlie, when scouting, if he got out of sight of the judges and gallery, was not above commanding Buck's dog or disturbing the other handler's dog, for example, or causing a bird to flush so that when the judges arrived, the brace mate was charged with a nonproductive. Buck, too, had his ways of gaining an advantage during a brace, if he could do it without getting caught. He was known to caracole or amble his horse sideways in an effort to signal his dog off trail or into likely bird cover or away from an honoring situation, although the more experienced judges were well aware of his tricks and kept a close eye on him.

Buck and Charlie's latest English pointer shared their bad reputation. He was a big, hare lipped, white dog with a dark red mask. His size was intimidating and his temperament ornery and mischievous, especially afield. His large, taut, muscular presence and protruding fang menaced most other dogs. A timid brace mate would keep its distance and give no challenge in a trial. On account of his mask, he was called Red Eyes. He was wolfish and devilish, and many handlers avoided Buck Arness because of him.

Not all dogs were intimidated by Red Eyes. A few hunted strong, hard, and fast against him, but these would often fall victim to his mischief. If he had the opportunity, out of sight of the judges, he'd steal a point, allowing his brace mate only the honor, that is, if the brace mate stood its original ground. A competitive dog might try to reestablish the primacy of its initial point, often getting caught by the judges, and then being disqualified for attempting to retake the stolen point that rightly belonged to it.

At the Kentucky state trials, Red Eyes ran against a promising pointer named Luke. Luke came on strong to a covey of quail just over a ridge and out of sight from his handler, the judges, and the gallery. As Luke made point, Red Eyes blindsided him from out of a parallel tree line and busted Luke's quail to flight, snarling a sinister laugh and leaving Luke standing confused. Red Eyes then followed the rousted birds down field to establish his own point. When the judges arrived, Luke, still standing, was charged with a nonproductive. He was picked up by his handler, who conceded the stake to Buck.

I know that this all attributes an intelligent malice to a brute, which you might fairly disbelieve, although I suspect that you found Melville's white whale true enough. Anyway, as I told you before, there is some fantasy in our tale, and there isn't much fable to a knight without there also being a dragon. Red Eyes, I suppose, wasn't born dragonish. Bad men likely made him that way. That's what Duke Arness would have said. Buck and Tall Charlie were such men, and they and Red Eyes were coming east.

SEVENTEEN

Tom and Mike spent the spring working on Rooster's steadiness. Although he had stood the birds he encountered that first day at Crooked Branch, he soon discovered the thrill of the chase. In those weeks that immediately followed, he would flush a bird to flight as soon as he caught scent of it and then make an always futile and often comical attempt to catch the fleeing bird midair. By early summer, though, his steadiness improved, and he would fairly hold his point through the flush and shot.

"Everything appears in good order," Tom said one day, "except for that darn flagging tail."

The flagging tail bothered Tom and, like I said, it is judged a fault.

"He's young and excited," Tom said one day. "He'll settle down once he understands that this is a business. I think maybe we can run him braced with another dog. Maybe he'll learn something by example. What do you say?"

"Well, sure, I'm all for it," Mike answered.

He turned to his brother, "Liam?"

"Sure." Liam, once bemused and skeptical, had grown fond of Rooster.

In that way, the summer months passed and Rooster learned the business end of field trialing by running in braces with the different dogs on Tom's string, Mike and Amy doing the handling. They had become good friends. Amy readily shared her knowledge of dogs and field trialing with Mike, and he was becoming a capable handler.

When Rooster was braced with Queen, it was as if she understood that he was just a novice. She even seemed to control her race in order to give Rooster the better opportunity to learn. "You follow me, young'un," she would say to him at the line. Then she would lead him along the course, teaching him the likely haunts of the quail among the brush and wildflowers or within isles of blue cedar, even into the now dense, summer green woods. Whenever she would go on point, Rooster would respectfully and attentively honor, as if studying her form and manners. She also seemed to let Rooster take the point on birds that she might otherwise have reached first, she being much quicker than he, conceding that perhaps he had scented the birds before her. "That's right, young'un, follow your nose," she'd say.

With Pokey, the two dogs were like kids in a playground . . . around a Maypole, on teeter-totters, up and down monkey bars and slides, all such as the summer time fields and woods afforded. Pokey never ran off from Roo, although she certainly might have. Instead, she kept a parallel course, and they each would seemingly call to the other, "Over here, let's look here," and they would change direction accordingly, appearing to take turns establishing point as the second to arrive would honor dutifully, even proudly, if not amiably. Often they would share points, like childhood teammates on a treasure hunt, a "divided find" it's called in the sport, neither dog getting the advantage.

When Rooster was braced with Chet, however, it was altogether a different story. "Eat my dust, flop ears," Chet would say to him at the break, and then off Chet would dash, leaving Rooster galumphing behind with his jack rabbit bounds. At first, Rooster would "tail" him, another trialing fault, and never would he find a bird of his own, thus always being obliged to honor Chet's points, often at a good distance, which I'm sure he found frustrating and embarrassing. Mike, too. "He'll learn," Tom said. And he ultimately did, taking his own courses, although still always to the rear of the faster pointer, and thus getting only limited bird contact, if any at all. It did not bode well for Rooster's future as a field trial competitor.

"He's a might too slow, that Rooster," Tom told Mike one day. "He'll never be able to compete against pointers and setters in horseback field trials. It doesn't matter that he's got a good nose, or that his manners are good . . . not if the other dogs beat him to the birds. In this game, nose and style are only part of the picture. A dog's got to run. Gotta run strong and long. He'll make a good hunting dog, though. He'll be a pleasure to hunt."

"Isn't there anything that I can do?" Mike asked, somewhat dejected.

"I don't hold too much hope," Tom shook his head slowly, "but you could try roading him, getting him some exercise to strengthen him and build his race. But, I don't know. He's a mongrel breed, like I told you. Back when I was your age, they would cull a dog like that."

Mike isn't the kind of kid to quit on an aspiration. "I'll think of something," he said.

For Mike, not-quitting isn't simply a matter of dogged determination. As a child, Mike had heard the cricket sing to Pinocchio. He has a tempered faith in the fancies of fortune; in shamrocks and wish bones, rabbits' feet and horseshoes, shooting stars and such. The sport of field trialing can be "dang fool frustratin' at times," Duke Arness had told a young Tom Quinn that summer way back when in North Dakota. Mike though, well, with a wink to the stars, Mike is the kind of kid who tackles frustrations head-on. "I'll think of something," he said.

EIGHTEEN

"What're you doing?" the butterfly asked Rooster, who was lying on his belly under the shade of a large oak at the far corner of our back yard.

"Hiding so I can get some rest," an exhausted Rooster replied tiredly.

"Why are you so tired?" the butterfly pressed.

"Because of Mike, he makes me road the whole day long, and do repeated fetches up hills and other exercises. He doesn't give me any time to just sit, except at bed time," Rooster yawned with one eye half closed. He directed the open eye to the butterfly, then he asked with a wrinkled brow, "And, where have you been lately, by the by?"

"Oh, I've been hanging around with some quail. You know? The ones I met that day at Crooked Branch. Nice folks…for birds. Downright humorous at times…had a good time. You've gotten pretty big these last couple of months there, Rooster. All that exercising must be working. Look at those muscles, those pecs and gluts and those biceps, um, um, um. Macho! What are you exercising for, anyhow?" the butterfly spoke while flitting about and examining Rooster from different vantage points, marveling at the apparent power of his thighs and the strength of his chest, his ribs accentuated.

"You've been with quail?" Rooster was surprised enough to open both eyes and raise his head. "That's what I've been doing. Mike takes me out to field trials, which involves finding quail…funny that I haven't seen you around." Rooster rolled over onto his back and stretched his legs skyward, and then he fell back to his side, both eyes drooping heavily.

"I've heard about those field trials from the quail. Fun and games, they say. How've you been doing? I've heard some pretty funny stories about some dogs." The butterfly answered and lit on Rooster's forehead peeking down at the closing eye lids.

"All right, I reckon. Matter of fact, I've placed in a number of trials lately, and Mike says that I might be entered in a championship someday." Rooster mumbled sleepily and did not lift his head.

Sparky came strutting over, "Who you talking to, Roo?"

"That blue butterfly there." Rooster sat up and the butterfly took wing.

"A butterfly, huh? Where're you from, butterfly?" Sparky intruded, his neck twisting and head spinning to catch the butterfly's rings of flight.

"She came with me from Mr. Mann's. She's just been away awhile. She's been staying with quail ... says she's learned some secrets about field trialing." Rooster answered for the butterfly.

"Oh...well, hey, we could use some secrets, huh, Roo? Might help in a championship...if you ever get in one, huh?" He jabbed Roo in the ribs and turned to the butterfly, "I'm Sparky. I'm his manager. So, tell me, what secrets do you know?"

The butterfly lit on the top of Rooster's head. "Oh, I've heard some things," she said, "those quail know the game pretty well. It's kind of like hide-n-seek with teams. The quail can be mischievous, though. They know how to bamboozle the dogs, if they want. Like if the dog scents a quail and goes on point, the quail can sneak off and burrow deep in the grasses before the handler arrives. When the handler goes to flush, he gets real frustrated 'cause he can't find the bird. I hear the quail gets a good giggle out of that one.

The quail can even shut off their scent, if they want. Sometimes they'll covey up so as to let off a lot of scent and attract a dog over their way, and then, as the dog approaches, they'll fan out into the tall grasses, borough down deep, and confuse the dog as to their whereabouts. Some dogs'll get dizzy just looking for 'em. Or, they'll shut off their scent until the dog is right on top of them. Then, when handler comes in to flush, they'll fly right up under the dog's nose, causing it to startle and break point. I even heard a story about how, a long time ago, I think it was in Georgia, one quail flushed and then it flew straight back down and pecked the pointing dog on its nose. They say that the dog didn't move, though. Held staunch, they say. A real good pointing dog, you bet. They're a funny bunch, those quail though . . . enough to make you laugh." The butterfly giggled.

"Well I'll be," Sparky grinned. "Did you know that about quail, Roo?"

"Can't say that I did, although I don't doubt it," Rooster shook his head wearily.

"Oh, it's true, but they know the rules of the game," the butterfly continued, "they pretty much will play fair most of the time. It's just once in awhile that they get impish, especially if they have a dislike for a dog or somethin' . . . they're all right ordinarily."

"I think maybe we should talk with them there quail," said the Big Spark. But, Rooster had fallen asleep. Sparky lay down on his belly beside him. He gazed off for a bit, and then he, too, napped, his chin across his outstretched left front leg. The butterfly fluttered off to our flower garden with its Catmint, Tickseed and Peonies. It was dusk.

NINETEEN

Rooster had a right to be tired. Mike had been working him pretty hard. It was paying off, though. Not just in Rooster's greater strength and stamina, but in his attitude as well. He began to show a new confidence that he exhibited when he was brought to toe the line at the break, like a prize fighter entering the ring. No longer would Chet bid him to eat dust, and they became friends, as hearty competitors often do.

Mike worked himself hard, too. Amy left home for her first year of college, and Mike took over Amy's responsibilities at Quinn Kennels, since he did not go away from home to school. He would help Tom as needed, like a hired hand. He learned while doing. It wasn't too long after Amy had left, that Mike was scouting for Liam at trials, and not long after that, Tom was letting Mike handle Tom's dogs in puppy and derby stakes.

Mike took a blue ribbon handling Tom's setter, Butter Cup, in a late October, New York derby stake. Butter Cup broke fast, ran strong, and dashed from one quail to another like a ball bouncing off the bumpers of a pinball game. She was the only dog in Tom's Kennel that placed that day, and Mike was pretty proud of himself. "You did fine, boy," Tom told him, and Liam agreed. "You're getting the hang of the sport and you're learning to read and understand a dog pretty well. That's a big part of this game, knowing the dog and what it's telling you as it runs its race. You're doing fine." Tom rested a hand on Mike's shoulder as they walked to the truck for the ride home at the end of the day. "Doing just fine," he said warmly.

But it was Rooster's new strength and confidence that gave Mike the most pride, especially because the competitors, judges, and galleries had begun to take notice. Early on, when Mike would bring Rooster to the line, there was a good bit of amusement, if not downright hilarity, at the site of the orange, floppy-eared dog with its pokey amble to the call. It was not unlike the ribbing Mike got when he first met Tom at Crooked Branch. And Tom would often hear his share of the ridicule, too.

"What'r ya bringing a mongrel dog like that to these stakes for, Tom?" someone would invariably ask. Tom wouldn't respond, except maybe with a nod of his head, or a tip of his cap, letting Rooster's race speak for itself. Sure, it was awkward in the beginning, but by the fall of Rooster's second year of competition, most people had seen or heard enough about that "orange mongrel dog" not to seriously question Tom anymore, although some good hearted jesting continued among his friends.

It was in that fall that Rooster placed first in the Robert Hollow Cup Stakes in western Pennsylvania. This is how the reporter described his run in *National Field Magazine:*

"Rooster, an orange dog of rare breeding, run out of the Quinn Kennel and handled by Michael Storey, was brought to the line looking completely out of place among the pointers and setters gathered for the stake, except that he had a confident carriage, his skin was tightly drawn against protruding ribs under a coarse coat, and his head was held high and to the forward with eager anticipation. Braced with Gun Smoke, a black and white pointer handled by Joe Connolly, the orange dog gave no ground on the break and was quickly to the fore, the gallery in a somewhat amused disbelief.

"The orange dog did not look back. He veered left along the piney tree line, disappeared within, only to just as quickly reappear to the front some hundred fifty yards up the trail, from whence he gave only a short, quick glance to his distant, rearward handler before cutting north across the trail and running strong off course, vanishing around the corner tree line of hemlock and oak, Gun Smoke all the while keeping a blazing pace to the front.

"Was the orange dog now lost? His scout, Liam Quinn, took leave as we reached the point of Rooster's diversion. Judge Carroll and handler held back to await the scout's report as Connolly and Judge Mane continued on course, the gallery along. As we followed the pointer, we heard the distant crack of the gun. Later, Judge Carroll would report the find of a small covey off course at six minutes, the orange dog staunch and steady, all in order.

"Until then, we attended the pointer as it ran strong to the fore and suddenly froze to a point. As handler and judge rode up to make flush, our attention was called to the reappearance of the orange dog rapidly cruising the crest of the rise above us on our right. The dog was running hard when it acknowledged the pointer on mark and came abruptly to a stop in honor, still above us some sixty yards away. Standing stout and strong, it appeared as like a wilderness scout or hunter in silent reconnoiters of the open fields below.

"Gun Smoke stood to the flush and was released, but the orange dog did not stir until its handler arrived and bid it "hie on," whereupon it launched into its charge, seemingly bent on overtaking the pointer that was now a good distance away to the front. We in the gallery slowed to allow ourselves to be overtaken, to best observe the performance of this unusual, flop-eared campaigner.

"The orange dog rushed passed us, but instead of continuing to the front in pursuit of the pointer, it crossed our intended course and sped off to our left into a copse of graying alder and yellowing birch. There it afforded us the opportunity to observe its manners on point as it marked a native grouse. We saw it intense and rock steady to the flush, wing and shot, all in order as scored by Judge Carroll, with its second find at thirteen, again off course, in further testament to its nose. There were better than thirty minutes and two thirds of the course remaining. How much more did this orange challenger, this Rooster, have to show us?

"We were not disappointed. After the grouse, the orange dog marked finds at nineteen, a bird apparently overrun by Gun Smoke, then again at twenty-six and thirty-seven. It then finished the stake strong to the front with plenty of run left in him for more. His five finds, all in perfect shooting dog order, with an electric intensity belied by his gangling appearance at rest, were two more than any other competitor and earned him the winner's blue ribbon. The placement was well deserved, and all applauded the judges' choice. We suspect that there is more to come from this unusual competitor."

TWENTY

"Did you read that there 'bout Tom Quinn?" Charlie Hinkle asked Buck Arness, tossing the copy of *National Field Magazine* on the sofa.

"Yeah, I read it," Buck sneered, walking in from the kitchen with a can of local *Muddy Missouri* beer in his hand. "Looks like old Tom has got himself a new breed of dog. Leave it to him. Couldn't succeed with a real dog, I reckon." Buck popped the can's flip top and began to drink his beer. He wiped dribble from his chin with his left hand, ignoring the grime.

"An orange mongrel, to boot," said Charlie. "Imagine that, huh. What kinda dog is that? Must have some kinda papers . . . they let it compete. I've got to get a look myself, before I believe what they writ there. Beat pointers and setters! That's bull, you ask me." Charlie paced as he spoke, one arm flailing to emphasize a point.

Buck sat on the sofa, put his drink down on the end table and picked up the paper. "Well, who'd it beat, anyhow? I only recognize a couple of the dogs in that stake. . .Bob Haskins' pointer bitch, Snow Blind. . .Jim Teague's pointer, High Falootin. . .a couple of others. . .Mike Walsh's setter. . .must be eastern dogs mostly. . .don't see much talent there. . .probably a fluke."

Tall Charlie looked over Buck's shoulder, "You remember that Gun Smoke dog, don't ya? Red Eyes run against him in Ohio a while back, remember? Wasn't a bad dog, especially? Red Eyes smoked him though. Remember how we laughed, 'Gun Smoke got smoked.' Har, har" Charlie stopped his pacing just long enough to look square at Buck for a reply.

"Oh yeah, I remember. As I recall, that dog got picked up for a nonproductive. Least wise there weren't no birds around by the time its handler went into flush. Funny how dogs have nonproductives when runnin' 'gainst Red Eyes, especially when you're scouting . . . huh, Charlie?" Buck looked up at Charlie with a crooked, yellow smile.

Charlie smiled back a gapped toothed grin, picked up Buck's drink, raised the can in a toast and then to his lips, and took a sip. Wiping his lips with the back of his free hand, he asked, "Dogs been fed?" He took another sip of the beer.

"Yeah, I fed 'em," Buck replied. "That Red Eyes is a strange dog, I'll tell ya. The other dogs is all curled up in their houses when I went out there. Not Red Eyes. He just paces back and forth in his kennel. It's like he never rests or sleeps. . .just like a machine that's always churning. He ain't normal, that dog. . .all strung out and high wired."

"He's a darn good dog. He'll get you that there championship is my bet," added Charlie, taking another sip from the can before Buck could grab it out of his hand. "Still, I'd take a long ride to see an orange dog. Can't see how a mongrel gets such 'knowledgement in our game. Next you know, they'll let poodles run. Haw! 'magine that will ya, a poodle, all puffy and such, toeing the line. Har!" He continued pacing as though it helped his imagination.

"Who knows, you may get to see that dog, if what's writ is fer truth," said Buck. "Maybe Ol' Tom will bring it round these parts. It'd be nice to see Tom Quinn agin…ask 'bout his hip. Heh? Him and his brother, what was his name. . .no, never mind. But who knows, might be we'll catch 'im up East; they hold the championship that way. Where is next year's championship, anyway. . .d'ya know?"

"Can't say I do. Look in the magazine, in the back, maybe."

"Well, hey, if it ain't in Virginia. Looks like maybe we just might be going east…Red Eyes qualifies. Wouldn't that be a kick. . .competing agin Tom Quinn and some orange mongrel dog? I don't suspect that that dog will qualify no how anyway. Who knows? Ain't no never mind. Can't say I really care."

Outside, in the cold Missouri night, a rain began to fall. The red masked pointer looked skyward defiantly then skulked into his doghouse, where he coiled into rest, his head outside the entranceway; chin down upon the muddy ground, unsheltered from the rain. He lay like that for only a moment then rose and left to renew his rectangular prowl of the kennel, spiteful of the weather.

PART THREE

FOR PETE'S SAKE

ONE

The short and chilly days of late autumn brought an end to training at Crooked Branch. We saw no more of Tom and Liam until Tom visited just before Christmas. He had a gift for Rooster, and he brought Pokie along. The young setter hadn't done so well in her fall trials, and Tom had taken to her mainly as a pet, although he had a mind to breed her at some point. Jan answered the door.

"Hello, I'm Tom Quinn. Is Mike home?"

With his yipping and yapping Sparky had already let the whole house know that someone was visiting, so I was on my way to the door when Jan opened it. I made the introductions. "Jan, this is Tom. . .Tom Quinn, the trainer that Mike's been working with. . .helped train Rooster."

"Oh. . .hello. . .it's very nice to finally meet you; I've heard so much… come in. Your dog can come in too, it's all right…Sparky won't bother her." She picked Sparky up. "You calm down," she scolded him with a tap on the nose, to which he responded with indifference. I yelled for Mike, "Hey Mike, Tom's here to see you." Then, shaking his hand, "Come on in…Pokey, too…Merry Christmas." I closed the door behind them.

Rooster had been out in the yard. He'd heard the commotion Sparky had caused and now was at the back door scratching and barking to come in. "Roo's out back," I told Tom, "Why don't we let these other two outside with him. They'll be all right, the yard is fenced;" which we did, to their obvious pleasure, Rooster and Pokey jumping and nipping at each other and then running off together, Sparky chasing, yipping and yapping at their heels all the way.

"Come on in," I said to Tom, leading him into the kitchen, Jan following. "Would you like a cup of coffee? Mike will be down in a. . ." but Mike appeared before I could finish. "Hey, Tom," he said, shaking Tom's hand, "Merry Christmas."

"Merry Christmas, Mike, I brought a present for Rooster." He handed Mike a small, wrapped gift. Mike peeled away the red foil to reveal a new, brown leather collar. A small, inscribed, brass plate was affixed just below the "D" ring. Mike read the inscription aloud, "Rooster 2008 Robert Hollow Cup Champion." "Wow," he said, showing and handing the collar to Jan, "That's just great. . .thanks Tom. . .that's really, really nice. . .really. . .I really appreciate it. Where's Roo?"

"He's out back," I said, receiving the collar from Jan as Mike went to call Rooster. "That's very nice of you, Tom," I said. Jan nodded in agreement, "Yes, very nice, thank you very much. Mike's really proud."

"That was a memorable day," said Tom. "I still can't believe that dog. Neither can most folks in the sport. It's like he's got some spirit in him that isn't apparent on the surface, he being pretty much a galoot by comparison with the pointers and setters he's staked against. Liam and I get a kick just seeing the faces on some people, although I guess we weren't much different when we first seen him. Your Mike is a good kid, too. It's been a real pleasure having them both around."

Rooster came hurrying into the house and upon seeing Tom he was pretty excited and glad happy, going right to him, tail wagging like a whirligig. Tom bent over to give him a hearty scruff and a scratch behind the ears. The other dogs came in right behind Rooster, and there was a general commotion, each dog seeking its own share of attention, Sparky jumping up at Jan to be picked up and held. Then, once lifted, peering down upon the others as if his higher berth reflected some superiority. I did earlier mention his Napoleonic complex, didn't I?

"Come here, Roo," bid Mike. "Tom brought you this new collar." Mike removed and replaced the old collar with the new one. "Pretty cool, huh? It says you're a champ." Rooster had no notion of the collar's newness or significance and just ran back over to Tom for some more petting. He had to squeeze Pokey aside, and she ambled over to Mike in substitution. "Hey Pokie," Mike greeted her, reaching down to scratch behind her ear.

"Winning that Hollow championship was no small feat, Mike," said Tom. "No sir, it was a big deal, Mike. Liam and I were talking, and we think Rooster's got what it takes…well he showed it. . .and we were thinking maybe to run him in some qualifying stakes for next year's championship. He'd only have to win or even be runner-up in just two stakes to qualify."

"Liam and I, we're thinking of going south for the winter. We got a friend in North Carolina with training grounds, and we're thinking of taking a couple of dogs down to get them ready for the spring stakes. We'd take Queeny and maybe one or two others. We were thinking maybe Rooster could come along."

"Rooster?" said Jan and I with simultaneous surprise.

"Well, Ed," Tom continued, turning to me, "Rooster has got what it takes to be a national champion. I know that may seem strange coming' from me, seeing as how I had my doubts early on, but he has shown some real talent for a mongrel breed. I think . . . Liam and I think . . . that he can do it if we work him over the winter months . . . give him the special attention that he needs.

"You'd take Roo? Well, gee . . . I don't know," I hesitated, "Jan? Mike?"

TWO

Tom took a sip of his coffee. "I can understand. You don't have to decide today. Liam and I won't be leaving until after the holidays. He'd be gone for a while . . . couple of months . . . be back round the end of March. I'd invite Mike, but I know he's got school. I know that you probably would miss Rooster, but that dog's got something and it sure would be something to see him do it. You don't have to decide today . . . think about it awhile."

"Well. . ." I started.

"You know, Ed, I've been at this sport all my life. Trained and competed with a lot of dogs . . . never got to the Invitational . . . might have once, years ago, before I fell and busted my hip. Maybe I'm being a bit selfish by asking you, but that Rooster . . . well, maybe Mike would let me come along with him, if Rooster can qualify. I know that I'll put my heart into training him. I believe . . . me and Liam . . . that he may just be able to do it."

"Well. . ." Again I tried to respond, although uncertain of what I might say.

"We'll take good care of him" Tom assured us, putting his coffee cup on the table.

"Oh, it isn't that, Tom. Jan? Mike? I don't know, Tom. We sure would miss him. Heck, it ain't just us either. I don't know what Sparky would do." I turned and mussed Sparky's hair. "Well, I don't know. Jan?" I looked from Tom to Jan.

"He's my dog, Dad," Mike interrupted, "I'm not all that sure either. But, you know, I've really come to enjoy this sport, and I've seen what Roo can do...puts his mind to it. Like Tom says, that was really something to see at that stake...him up on that hillside standing tall in honor. It was like he had a spirit in him or something, some star shine. I don't know. I want to think about it. Imagine going to an Invitational . . . with Rooster . . . I don't know."

"Wait a minute, I've got a say in this; he's my dog, too, you know." Jan interjected as she put Sparky down; but he clamored to get back up, pawing at her and then at me. I picked him up. Jan continued. "I know what you two guys may be thinking. I've got a say in this, too. Who's the one who feeds him every day? I don't know about not having Rooster around for a couple of months."

"Tom, we'll talk it over. I appreciate your thoughts. I understand. We'll talk. Jan, Mike, we don't have to make up our minds right now. Tom's not leaving for a while yet. We can think it over and let him know later."

"I don't need to think about. . ." Jan began, but Mike interrupted.

"He's my dog, guys. I'm the one who has been training him and running him. I'm thinking that I've put a lot of work into this, not just with Rooster, but with Tom and Liam and with field trialing and everything. What did I do all that for? If Tom and Liam think that there is a chance that Rooster could compete in some national championship, well, it wouldn't be just Rooster who was doing it; it would be me, too. I did all this work. Who knows if I'd ever get another chance or have another dog, or that I'd even want another dog? Tom's been doing this for years and has had all kinds of dogs. This might be my only chance ever."

"Mike, Tom's gotta go. We can all talk about this later on. Take our time. We'll see. Tom, I'll call you and let you know."

THREE

Spring came early, after a mild winter, so that March saw the return of the robins. The butterfly returned, too.

"Hey Sparky, what ya doin laying there?"

"Nothing."

"Where's Roo?"

"He's been gone."

"Really? Where to?

"Tom took him somewhere down south to train . . . Carolina or someplace."

"Geeze, I wish I had known. I was down that way, myself. You know, south for the winter. I'd have looked him up. Training with quail again, huh? Plenty of quail in them Carolinas."

"I guess. I ain't been too happy with him gone, so I hope *he's* had a good time."

"When's he comin' back?"

The question was put just as they heard the back door shut. Turning, they saw Rooster standing upon the deck. He stood tall, and straight and I guess that you'd say statuesque. Sparky stood to look, but only for a moment. Both dogs then broke into a run towards each other, Rooster down from the deck with a bound, Sparky just as quick as his little legs could motor. They came together almost like charging bulls, Sparky tumbling over in the collision, then bouncing back up and leaping and pawing at Rooster, who pawed back and nuzzled; then he stopped and he stood erect. He looked different.

The butterfly flew over and fluttered around, examining Rooster from tail to muzzle. "My, my . . . how you've changed. What have they been feeding you, Rooster!? Look at him, Sparky! He looks. . .how you call it. . .really fit. . .not like the pokey dog I remember. . .kinda like. . .I don't know…"

"A caballero!" said Sparky.

"Huh?"

"A Spanish knight . . . a Spanish horseman, a cavalier in the old Spanish West, like when there were cowboys. Hey, Roo, draw!" Sparky jumped back and bent at the haunches as if challenging Rooster to "go for his gun."

Rooster stood staunchly still, turning only his neck toward the Big Spark. "I missed you guys," he said.

We stood and watched this reunion from our back porch, Mike and I. "It was worth sending him to Carolina with Tom," Mike said, "although I missed him." "Yeah, we all missed him," I added. "Tom believes Rooster can now compete with the best of the shooting dogs, or so he says," Mike continued. "He's entered us in a stake next week, in New York. I may have to miss a day of school. That's okay, right?" I smiled at him. "Ask your mom." "Ma," he turned and hollered toward the house.

FOUR

"Did you see that?" Tall Charlie was speaking to Buck Arness as Buck entered the house stamping his shoes at the door step. His left shirt sleeve hung loose with a ragged tear.

"See what?" Buck snarled.

"That orange dog of Tom Quinn's won another stake. . .the Sloan Shooting Dog stake up there in New York. . .says so here in *National Field*. . .March 25. Dang! That dog just may be fer real. What d'ya thinks of them apples? That was a qualifying stake. Says he beat nineteen other dogs, and they was all pointers and setters…well there was a shorthair in there too, but they don't count, heh."

"Didn't see it. You know I was out with the dogs. Don't say it matters all that much. Good for Tom Quinn. Red Eyes' last stake in that rag, too?" Buck was in a foul mood.

"Nope, must not have been submitted in time. You know that Dick Chaffee. He's a good reporter, all right, but he don't get his reports done none too quick…maybe next week."

"No never mind. Red Eyes got a qualifier, too. Who knows, maybe we're heading for a showdown. We'll see. There beer in the fridge?" Buck tramped towards the kitchen.

"Yeah, there's a couple. I'll have to make a run later." Charlie was pacing with the rolled newspaper in his hand, waving it up and down with the rise and fall of his arm.

He swatted a fly against a window, adding but a bit to its smoky film from the wood stove.

Buck opened the fridge and came back tapping the top of a beer can with his right index finger. He kept tapping as he walked to look out of the front window. The sun had just begun to set. It was orange on a gray sky. He turned to Tall Charlie, who had walked up behind him.

"Red Eyes got in a tangle with Clanton. That Clanton's got as much gumption as Red Eyes and don't back away none neither. Red Eyes don't take no lip and won't back off no challenge. . .specially during a run. He's mean like a junk yard dog when he's running. Clanton tried to steal his point, and Red Eyes went right after him. Good thing I wasn't too far off. I had to pull 'em apart and got bit on my arm. . .damn cur. I let him have it but good. He don't give a damn. What a dog. If he weren't winnin' I'd get rid of him." Buck took a gulp of beer.

"No place you could put 'im Buck. Who else would want a dog like that 'cept you? Your dad warned you long ago about red marked dogs…dogs with a red mask like Red Eyes. Didn't old Fuzz say they had the devil in 'em. You got a devil dog, Buck." Charlie put the paper on the edge of an end table. It unfurled and fell to the floor.

"He'd be culled sure as if he were a worthless pup, I'll tell you that. I'm too old for a dog like that. Getting too old as it is, now. I just want that trophy 'fore I go. He'll get it for me." Buck insisted.

"You got trophies enough." Charlie tried to be consoling.

"Them was with my dad's dogs. . .or their get. Well, he's dead now, and it's my turn. I've been snake bit my whole dang life. Red Eyes is my breeding, and I'll be damned if he don't do right by me." Buck did not want to be consoled.

"I see he left you bloody. Want a bandage?" Charlie was solicitous, but not compassionate. Empathy surely wasn't his nature.

Buck turned to look back out the window. He wiped a film of stove smoke from the glass with his torn shirt sleeve. "Yeah, he tasted my blood alright. Look at him out there prowling his kennel. He wants something, that dog. Maybe now that he's tasted my blood he'll want what I want. We'll get it, boy…just a bit longer, but it's comin'…this fall…in Virginia. We'll get it. Damned if we don't."

FIVE

THE NATIONAL FIELD MAGAZINE

The Field Trial Magazine of America

St. Louis, Saturday, April 23, 2009

Pennsylvania Open All-Age Championship

THE Keystone Field Trial Club held the thirty-third running of the Pennsylvania Open All-Age Championship at the Otter River Wildlife Management Area on April 2–4. The Judges were John Furman of Binghamton, N.Y. Mike Purvis of Wellsville, Penn., and Alvin Melly of Point Pleasant, W.V. Our thanks to the judges and to the club members who helped make this event a success, particularly Mildred Gribbs, who served as both marshal and field reporter. Without Mildred's faithful notes, this report would be no more than a list of winners and also-rans.

Friday morning broke with the promise of good weather for the weekend. The April chill misted the breath of men, horses and dogs. The air was scented with the smoke of morning campfires and carried the sounds of scurrying. Those scents, later enhanced by the smells of dinner fires, and those sounds, with the added yips of dogs, the banter of men and the snorts and whinnies of horses, would continue throughout the weekend. The meet would end Sunday evening with an awards dinner, and with two dogs from the Massachusetts kennel of Tom Quinn taking both winner and runner-up ribbons.

Forty-four dogs were entered, and ten were called back for the finals on Sunday. Before proceeding with my report of Sunday's braces, I must mention the loss of Timberlake's Lumber Jack on Friday. Jack, owned by Sam Richardson of West Falls, Ohio, broke strong in the third brace on Saturday, was seen running east off course into the hardwoods, and then not seen again. The scout was sent, but after a time he returned to report the dog lost. Sam then quit the race to go with the scout in search of the pointer. After several hours they returned without success. They took to their truck to course the frontage roads, and several others joined them.

By night fall the dog still had not been found, and an alert was placed with the local game warden. It wasn't until late Saturday afternoon that the warden appeared with the pointer crated in his truck. The dog was lame, but it did not appear to be serious. Jack had been the prerace favorite, and his prospects for the Invitational were believed to be very good. This was a very sad misfortune for Sam. We wish him and Jack the best. Now, to report on Sunday's braces:

Otter River sits atop the Allegheny Plateau and presents challenging grounds for the running of a field trial. The course breaks in a quarter mile narrow sided by northern hardwoods and white pine, then opens onto reclaimed coal fields of tall sedge, wild rye and switch grass, with copses of cedar, maple and beech. It is natural grouse country, and dogs can be put to the test on both the native and the planted birds, for the latter of which we used quail. The land rises and dips with sometimes steep, shale hills over which the dogs disappear, and down which horse and rider tread cautiously because of the loose footing.

Ken Hilton's pointer, King's Ran Some, was paired with Don Fisher's pointer, Belle Bottoms, in the first brace, and Ran Some would set the bar for all the dog's thereafter. This pointer took a rocket launch off the break and was very quickly gone from sight over a hill top as if in orbit over the horizon. Belle broke in a veer to the right and could be eyed in that general direction all the while that the gallery pursued Ran Some's line. As the female observed our course, she came around and crested the hill top before us. As we reached the top in the field below us, we espied Ran Some on point. Then Belle, so completely out of character, failed to honor. Fisher and scout rode her down, her day done, while Hilton went in to flush, everything in order. Ran Some continued a strong solo race with three more all-in-order finds, and that set the mark to beat.

The mark would not stand long, however, as Tom Quinn's setter, Queen, took the break in the second brace alongside Willie Collin's pointer, Long Legged Sam. Queen had been much talked about after her first race, and she would not disappoint in the finals. We first found her on point at 15 by the Kettle River that runs the early part of the trail on the east. Continuing to the east, she quickly had her second find, a native, at 25 along the hardwood edge. Meanwhile Sam had an early nonproductive and otherwise did not please his handler and Collins leashed him. We continued on behind Queen, who at 40 held point on a small covey in tall sedge and rye. The flush went up, and the dog stood regally, her feathered tail wisped by the breeze. It was a pretty sight. Queen had her fifth find at 55, again all in order, and she finished the race as strong as she had begun it, ceding to the handler's call. After this, only her kennel mate would later present a challenge to her crown.

Darrel Bennett's pointer, Harley, and Erin Stile's pointer, Gunner, made up the third brace. Both are strong running dogs with more than several titles among them, Harley having won this Championship last year. They demonstrated their winning styles throughout their sixty minutes on the ground; unfortunately, their bird work was lacking. Harley's first was at 25, with a second ten minutes later, while Gunner was empty until 40. Perhaps indicative of their similarities, they shared a find at 50. It was an appreciated performance but not enough to overcome Queen and Ran Some, the leaders to that point.

Jimmy Boren and Nate Downs brought their muscular pointers, DJ and Rockabilly, respectively, to the line for the fourth brace. The pantingly eager dogs broke strong and ran hard in parallel lines, simultaneously cresting the first rise. As we crossed, we found DJ on point with Rockabilly in honor, and the flush was handled all in order. The scene was reversed shortly thereafter, as the dogs continued to run in a tandem not often seen in this sport. Following that flush, Downs handled Rockabilly in a wide swing to the west a good stride, and the dogs hunted independently from then on, DJ with an all in order find in the grasses at 40, and Rockabilly making staunch point at 49 within a cedar copse. Both dogs finished very well in the judges' estimation.

The last brace brought Quinn Kennel's second entry, Rooster, handled by Mike Storey, with Liam Quinn at scout. The brace mate was Ike Copeland's Rebel Run, a big all white pointer out of Clyde's Rebel and Copeland's Whisper of Wind, a championship breeding. Although the orange Rooster dog, a rare breed, had done well enough to earn its place in the finals, not much was expected of it in competition with the Copeland dog, especially in consideration of the young age of its handler. We would be surprised from the moment the young handler bid his charge "hie on."

To be sure, Rebel Run out paced the orange dog at the break and indeed was soon gone from sight, but Rooster had an unexpected speed to his run and was not behind without purpose, coming to an early point almost at the same spot along the Kettle River as its kennel mate had done earlier. His handler appeared to show urgency as he rode to the dismount quickly, flushed quickly and recast quickly, all as if the clock were his only competition. The dog went right to task. It stayed along the course of the river. In less than five minutes, it was again on point, and all handled at a fast pace, but in good order. This time Storey handled the dog away and back to the main trail where it would now be behind the birdless Rebel.

The orange dog's two finds within twenty minutes had given him the leg up, but now running behind Rebel, his next bird work would be an honor, and Rebel's speed suggested that was how the Quinn dog would end the day. But Storey stepped off the trail to the right and the orange dog seemed to read the meaning, coursing off Rebel's lead and into its own hunting grounds. He found his third and last bird at 45, while Rebel had but one more find. As both dogs ended strong, everything was now up to the judges.

And the 2009 Pennsylvania Open All-Age Champion is Quinn's Queen, in the judges' opinion the class of the heat. Runner-up went to the other Quinn entry, the orange Rooster. The dog's three finds and staunch honor, coupled with an intelligent and strong race earned him the nod over rest of the pack. While there may have been some among the competitors who questioned a result that gave runner up to a "mongrel breed," none among the gallery who observed the dog's run could voice any reservations, and the judges were comfortable in their decision. Congratulations to Tom Quinn.

Now I will report on the events of the preceding days, knowing that many appreciate hearing the call on their dogs, even though they were not brought back for the finals....

SIX

The June 14 edition of *The National Field Magazine* reported the May win of Red Eyes at the Arkansas Classic, another qualifying race. But no one at the Quinn Kennel paid the news any mind. They were all too busy. There had been a litter of pointer pups born at the kennel in late February, and while the puppies were still too young for any serious training, they demanded their share of attention, especially when let loose in the Crooked Branch fields. Fortunately, Amy was home from school for the summer, and she enthusiastically took responsibility for the brood. At the same time, she showed a special interest in Rooster and his prospects for the National Invitational.

Mike was with Amy at Tom's farm on an early June, sky-blue morning of wispy white clouds and the green smell of late spring. They were with the puppies in the old, faded and peeling red barn with its floor of scattered yellow hay.

"That's really great that you get to compete in the Invitational, Mike."

"Yeah, pretty good, huh? Rooster going to the Invitational, no one would have thought that . . . especially me. You helped a lot. You know? You really did."

"Well, it's great." Amy bent down and picked up one of pups. "I imagine it will be a long time before I'll ever get to the Invitational, what with school and all. Who knows, though, by the time this puppy is of age, he might just be the one to take me there . . . if Tom doesn't sell him." She lifted the puppy up to her face, shook it teasingly, and brought its forehead down to hers. They rubbed noses.

"Which one is that?" Mike had not yet figured out how to tell the puppies apart exactly, they all being white with black markings here and there.

"This one is Pete," replied Amy. "You can tell by the one black ear." She turned the dog towards him. "Tom says it reminds him of his first dog. Tom's got all kinds of memories, but he talks about that first dog the most, even though it wasn't one of his best, that one and Deputy...the one that almost won him the National in Alabama . . . the day that Tom broke his hip. Did he ever tell you about the time that a quail flew back and pecked Deputy on the nose, and Deputy just stood there and held his point, stone still like a marble statue? Or, was it Pete that did that? I'm not sure, now, one of them. It was long ago. Some in the game still talk about it. Was it Deputy or Pete? I can't remember."

"No sir, really, that's hard to believe? Would a quail really do something like that? I've never seen them do anything except fly away in a brown flurry. You're kidding me, right?" Mike was unsure of Amy. She had been away at school and there was a hint of estrangement not fully concealed by the warmth with which she first greeted him, or by the slight kiss that she had softly planted on his cheek.

"Well, I guess you have to hear Tom tell it. Tom says that there are two sides to the business of training and running field trial dogs. There's the reality, which can be black and white, and sometimes even a dark gray like storm clouds, and then there's the fantasy. The fantasy isn't so much make-believe, as it is what you *want* to believe." She charmed Mike with a slight smile and wink.

Amy put the puppy down and it dashed off to play among its litter mates. "See," she turned to Mike with a gentle smile, "Tom grew up hearing stories about leprechauns and forest sprites and pots of gold at the end of rainbows. Tom may have had some hard knocks along the way, but he has never really wanted *not* to believe. I think that Rooster has given Tom something to believe in, something that is far enough removed from reality to be fantasy... a big galoot of a loping, orange dog with floppy ears and yellow eyes, running against powerful pointers and stylish setters in field trials." Her smile brightened at the thought. "Well, if you can believe that, then you can believe in leprechauns. And, if Rooster is real, then leprechauns are real, and Tom can be secure in his hopes and dreams, which is a good thing, for an old Irish like Tom. It's what hopes and dreams are made of."

"Well..." Mike turned from the puppies to Amy, "I guess we'll just have to see if we can't make Tom's dreams a reality. Will you scout for me at the Invitational?"

"You're kidding?" Amy began to walk from the barn.

"No, really, I mean, you know this game better than me. Liam has been my scout. I don't think that he would mind, since he gets to scout for Queen in the Invitational, if Tom handles her like he says that he's going to." Mike followed Amy with a plaintive enthusiasm.

"Wow, Mike that would really be great. But, I don't know . . . not with school and all." Amy was hesitant. Seeing Mike again after so many months awoke a forgotten tenderness. She was not frail with shyness, but she felt a need to better understand her feelings before making any kind of a commitment.

"It will be in the early fall . . . in late September . . . and it will only mean missing school for a couple of days and a weekend, maybe a Monday, too. You would miss school if you were in college sports or something. Well, this is a sport. I'm going to have to miss school, too." Mike pressed.

"Well . . . I have to think about it, and the travel, too. But I would like to help you train Rooster this summer, if you want. Then, we'll see. Who knows?" They walked along together sharing stories of the past months they had spent apart, but none of that seemed to really matter. The day that they first met at Crooked Branch, that day when their eyes first met, was like yesterday.

Half way across the country, in Missouri, at dusk, Buck stood outside of Red Eyes's run, his hands gripping the galvanized gate, his forehead pressed hard against it. "You're taking me to the Invitational, dog. You're gonna get me that trophy, and damn you if ya don't."

An indifferent Red Eyes prowled his kennel like a zoo tiger.

SEVEN

The summer heat is hard on dogs, so you train early in the morning or early in the evening, grateful for the longer days. In between the orange rising sun and the red setting sun, the dogs are kenneled, and their handlers take to their other chores or responsibilities.

The summer of 2009 was different for Rooster and Queen. Tom was worried that a September Invitational in Virginia might mean runs in the heat of a Southern day. He wanted to make sure that stamina would not be an issue for either of his charges, so he ran them the proverbial morning, noon, and night. "We don't know what water there will be along the course," he noted his concern. "We'll carry canteens, and I would expect that the grounds will have half barrels at points along the course, but I mean to have our dogs well-conditioned."

Tom was also concerned about Mike's handling in the Invitational, Mike being only a novice. To be sure, Mike had performed well enough in the races he ran. He showed a good feel for the game. It was Mike's idea to hurry his flushes. "I figured Rooster isn't as fast as most dogs he's braced with, and I figured maybe it would help, if I sped things up a bit," he told Tom. It was a good idea, thinking to beat the clock. Cutting time off the flush would help to keep Rooster from always trailing his brace mate and being defaulted into honors.

Still, there was a lot for Mike to learn in order to compete against the professionals who would be handling dogs at the Invitational. Tom's concern was heightened by the thought that Amy might be Mike's scout. "Those two kids will be gobbled up by some of those handlers," he cautioned Liam, "Wild Bill Crossley, Big Lou Ponti, those guys, Canada Sam Baio, too. You know that. Rooster might be as good a dog as any. Handling will determine the outcome. We have to make sure those kids are ready, Liam."

Mike was given books to read, something he usually had little interest in doing during the summer. He needed to understand more than just the point and flush of field trialing. "This isn't just about following a dog around in the bird fields," Tom emphasized, "If you want to win, you need to know what you are winning and why it is important…not only to you, but to the sport of the pointing dog." Mike read, and he learned, but the real learning came in the fields.

Tom had Mike handle every dog in the Quinn Kennel, including Queen. Mike would run in braces with Amy. One day he would handle one dog and she the other, next day they'd switch, even with Rooster. Liam always accompanied Mike, explaining a dog's performance, the peculiarities of any situation, how to improve the one and to address the other.

"You can't be caught with a nonproductive, Mike," Liam warned. "You have to know how to read the dog's point. You can tell from the way the dog carries its head or from its body language, in what direction or how far away the bird may be. Never initially approach the dog from the front . . . always from the rear and to the side. Move along that path as far to the front as you suspect the bird may be . . . stir that ground with your boot . . . then come back towards the dog, sweeping the ground as you go. The idea is to get out in front further than you estimate the bird to be. You don't want to fail to produce a bird, Mike, and you don't want to waste a lot of time doing it. The judges won't be too tolerant if you don't produce the bird quickly."

Horsemanship was another area where Mike needed improvement. He had to learn to amble his horse at a pace so that he would not be left behind by the other handler trying to keep the brace mate to the front. "There's another trick you have to learn," Tom told him as he coiled a long lead. "You have to be able to sidestep your horse off course to get your dog away from trailing a faster brace mate…without the judges thinking that you're controlling the dog's natural run. Sort of like what you did in the Pennsylvania Open. I call it a caracole, although it ain't really. Amy will teach you."

Each day, when the training was done, Mike and Amy would go riding. She took him on wooded paths, canopied in the oak green fullness of the summer, where horse and rider would need to negotiate obstacles of fallen limbs or low hung branches. Then, out onto broad fields of tall grasses and wild flowers, in July purple with fringed orchids, fireweed, loosestrife, and steeplebush, in August yellow with sow thistle, goat's beard, sneezeweed, and coneflower, here and there Black-Eyed Susans wiggled in the wind. Once in the fields they would push the horses to a pace approaching a canter. Always Amy would look back to check Mike's horsemanship, and always she smiled.

Their ride would end on the crest of a hill above where the small river at Crooked Branch flowed at its widest. There, they would dismount and hobble the horses. They might walk a bit, test the water with their toes, skip a stone or occasionally just sit and listen to the stream babble over its crimson and amber pebbled bed. A wood thrush might warble as the sun was slowly tucked beneath thin, wrinkled sheets of white cloud that turned a primrose pink as they unfolded over the horizon. Dreamily dawdling on horseback in the reverie of the soft summer evening, they would make their return before nightfall. And, always she smiled.

Mike told Amy that Jan and I planned to rent a RV and to go to the Invitational, as we had never seen Mike or Rooster compete in a field trial.

"Sparky, too?" she asked.

"Sparky, too." he nodded.

EIGHT

Toward the end of the August, Mike invited Amy to join him when he took Rooster for a swim.

"Yup, he swims like a fish," he told her. "Every so often, I take him up to a large pond in the woods where my cousin, Sam, has some property just northwest of here a bit. It's pretty and isolated, quiet. Sam leaves a canoe there, and I paddle around while Rooster swims. It's a real good exercise for him. He can swim for a long time . . . over an hour, easy. There's room for two in the canoe, and for Sparky, too."

Amy was excited. "Sure, I would love to go, when?" she asked.

"This Saturday afternoon, I'll pick you up around two. Okay?"

She blushed shyly and nodded enthusiastically, and he responded with a wide smile, "Great!"

Cousin Sam's property was more remote, and the pond much deeper in the woods, than Mike may have suggested. The steep, wooded land was up in the northern end of the Berkshire Mountains, close to the Vermont border, and the pond well over a mile's hike from the trailhead where the kids parked the Jeep, on the gray gravel shoulder of a winding, old country road. They arrived at the pond a little later in the afternoon than Mike had initially intended. But the path to the pond was clear, and Mike wasn't too concerned that they might still be hiking out of the woods after dark, especially since the moon had only begun to wane from its mid-August fullness.

Running ahead of Mike and Amy, Rooster and Sparky were the first to reach the lily padded pond. The faded orange canoe lay topside down not far from the shore, just outside of the fringe of the blue rushes and the cattails at their full, late season height with their deep, brown stalks. Both dogs stood for a moment at the water's edge. Then Rooster entered the pond, wading in up to his knees. Not the Big Spark, though. He's afraid of water.

"It's really nice here, Mike, so quite and private." Amy enjoyed the peace of the deep woods and the serenity of the pond as it rippled softly in a gentle breeze. She quietly inhaled the woody air infused with hints of water lily and aquatic iris.

"Come on; help me turn the canoe over," Mike roused her from her reverie.

As Mike reached down to lift the canoe, a frightened, black and yellow ribbon snake slithered quickly away, causing both kids to start and then smile at each other's timidity. They flipped the canoe and then pushed it to the pond's edge, settling it halfway into the water. Rooster turned his neck to watch. Sparky yipped and danced about on the shore as if he were directing the activities.

Amy entered the canoe and took a seat at the bow. Mike handed a fidgeting Sparky to her, and then he removed his sneakers and shoved the canoe further into the water before climbing in himself at the stern. Using a paddle, he gave a last prying push to release the canoe from its hold of the shore. Amy set Sparky down. He curled at her feet and she and Mike paddled away. Rooster followed.

"He really swims!" Amy was surprised. "Look at his tail wag; it's spinning like a propeller. That's hilarious. He must really be enjoying himself."

"Oh, he'll swim all day." Mike answered. "Hey, look over there. See them? The turtles, there, on that dead tree limb protruding from the water? There are several of them. They're sunning themselves." He gestured with the oar still in his hand.

"Look, Rooster is swimming over that way," Amy pointed.

As Rooster approached, the turtles slipped into the water. A small, green and yellow head then surfaced a short distance away, then another elsewhere nearby. Rooster swam towards the first, and when it dove beneath the surface, he swam around in small circles in search of it, and then he swam off towards the other. This game of "Marco Polo" continued as the canoe slid quietly past. Then Mike called Rooster to come along, a call that Sparky echoed with scolding barks of yips and yaps.

The kids soon reached the further part of the pond, their approach causing a mallard couple to take flight. A frog splashed from a lily pad, as the canoe brushed the cattails aside and slid with a scrape onto the shore stirring the pond's muddy bottom into a watery cloud. Amy lifted Sparky out of the boat and he barked to Rooster to hurry, but Rooster paid Sparky no mind and swam to a different beachhead, shaking vigorously when he made shore. His short, coarse, orange coat would quickly dry.

NINE

"Come on, Amy, I want to show you something," Mike turned from the canoe towards the woods. There was no clear path to Mike's objective, and as he pushed ahead he swept aside laurels, chokeberries and other shrubs, brush and brambles to clear the way for Amy and Sparky as they followed. Rooster would make his own way to the front, veering from side to side.

"Look there," Mike pointed, "isn't it neat? It's mica. Ever see such a big stone of it? You can peel slices from it. Look." Mike reached down to the stone and pulled away a small sheet of the shiny and flakey mineral. He briefly held the paper thin slice up to his eye, and then he passed it to Amy. "You can almost see through it. I've heard that it was sometimes used for windows in the olden days, in colonial times."

"That's really cool, Mike," Amy remarked as she held the translucent slice of stone before her eyes and turned to face the sun. The sun's rays diffused through the milky mineral pane. She next turned towards the pond, and then down to look at Sparky, and she smiled with amusement at the distorted image of the little, black dog leaping at her feet. She returned the slice of stone to Mike, who put it in his shirt pocket, and they went back towards the shore of the pond, where Mike sat down on a fallen tree. Amy stood a while, as if breathing in the both time and space, and then she joined him on the log.

"What are your dreams, Mike?" She asked softly and, as she spoke, she gazed up through the tree tops that filtered the light of the westward sun, as if her own dreams might reside there, then back into his brown eyes inquiringly.

Mike turned to her and smiled tenderly, he twisted a reed around his finger. "Well, I don't dream much about things, Amy. I mean, I don't think too many fanciful thoughts, not like about the future and stuff. When I'm at a place like this...when there's a clear, blue sky and those curled white clouds and everything is reflected in the water, even the pines along the shore...that's like a dream, for me." He bent and picked up a stone that he skipped across the pond, the ripples splashing then gently, dreamily swaying the blue, white and evergreen reflections. "And, you, sitting here with me, too."

She took one of his hands into hers. He looked into her green eyes, which, like the pond, sparkled with reflected sky. They kissed… softly, nervously, unsure of themselves. Then, suddenly, the moment was broken by challenging growls and sharp, loud and frantic barks, and the panicked, unmistakable yips and yaps of the Havanese.

"Where are the dogs!?" Mike and Amy started and rose in unison.

Mike raced toward the commotion and quickly came upon Rooster and Sparky in a fearful confrontation with a frightening, ash gray coyote, its ferociously bared fangs glistening with spittle. Rooster was standing courageously, dauntingly firm legged, strong and stout. Sparky would step forward pugnaciously with challenging growls, only to immediately leap back behind Rooster with a high pitched yelp. The coyote eyed the little dog with a menacing, hungry glare through flashing black eyes. Mike yelled for the dogs to come away, but they stood their ground with defensive determination.

Amy came up behind Mike. At first they shared a frantic glance, and then Amy bent and picked up a fist size stone that she hurled powerfully at the coyote, hitting it hard upon its flank and knocking it forcefully to the ground with a huffed yelp. "Scat varmint," she hollered, as she bent to pick up another stone. The coyote rose with a stumble, and then ran off without a sound, returning a vengeful scowl across its shoulder. Amy threw another stone as the coyote disappeared into the shade of the woods. Sparky made as if to give chase, but he stopped at Mike's command, happy for the restraint, I'm sure, and then he returned and stood at guard by Amy's feet. Rooster did not move and had never flinched throughout the confrontation.

The day was darkening. "We had better leave," Amy turned to Mike, who looked at her bewildered. "Third base, varsity softball," she answered his bewilderment with a confident smile. She picked up Sparky as she turned to the shore.

They quickly paddled the canoe to its base, both dogs aboard as there was no time for Rooster to swim at his leisure. After beaching the canoe, they began a hurried return to the car, the day fading quickly into brown dusk, the path all the darker in the forest shadows. They came to the roadside as the sun was giving its last light, its surrender to the dark accompanied by a distant and defiant howl.

It was a quiet ride home. They briefly, tenderly, held hands.

TEN

That evening, lying in bed, Amy mused over the day. She smiled to recall the look on Mike's face when she shooed the coyote with a stone, and she flattered herself. She couldn't wait to tell Tom and Liam. Her mother didn't understand. Her mom just lectured her about being off in the woods after the dark. "And what about bears?" her mom demanded, "You couldn't shoo away a bear with a stone, Amy."

She thought of Rooster and Sparky, that brave little Sparky, the Big Spark. He might have been that coyote's dinner, she smiled. But, not if Rooster could help it, her smile broadened; but, I'm glad that I was there. Mike could have done it, too, I know, she reflected. There's no way that Mike would have allowed his dogs to be harmed without a fight, fist or stone, she was sure. But, otherwise, she was unsure about Mike.

She had known him for almost two years now. They were friends, certainly. But, their friendship was pretty much confined to dog training, always with Tom and Liam about. Even those late summer afternoons, when they rode off together to sit and dabble at the edge of the Crooked Branch stream, were merely the jaunts of playmates. No, she wouldn't use that word. Simply "friends" would be more like it. And, we're soon to be adults, after all, or at least we're going to college soon, she reminded herself.

She recalled the day Mike first arrived at Crooked Branch, he and that floppy eared, orange, mongrel breed of a dog of his, just a puppy then, like him, just a kid, like her. She smiled at the thought of her first impressions of both the boy and his dog. Even though the dog garnered the greater attention from Tom and Liam, and, well, from her too, still, she couldn't help but to be more curious about Mike that day. Who was he? What was he like? He was kind of cute with his longish, unkempt brown hair and blue eyes, and his funny dog. Then, suddenly, she was riding with him, following his floppy eared, orange dog through the early spring meadow grasses, over the knoll, Mike comically awkward astride a horse, and he still can't ride well, she shook her head with a smile, into the woods where the dog unexpectedly, totally unexpectedly, she recalled, pointed a bevy of quail and then allowed her to flush, steady to the shot. He's a good dog, that Rooster, she smiled.

Next thing she knows, there they are on a date, and it was a date, too, hiking in the woods, canoeing on a pond. And, they sit, and Mike says something about dreams, and about her, and they kiss, not a real kiss, not really, just a playmate's kiss, a first kiss. Well, maybe it was something more, we are adults, after all, or it might have been, but for that dang cur coyote. I hope I hurt him good for scaring the dogs and causing such a commotion like he did. It was a good throw, huh, she preened.

But, it wasn't the kiss that caused the wrestling among her emotions. During the ride home she and Mike had held hands. Only briefly, okay, but with a tenderness that coursed through her, through her fingers and through her arms and into her chest where it produce a sigh that flushed her cheeks and moistened her eyes, and she wanted to look at him, but she couldn't.

Now, as she lay there, she just didn't know. She turned on her lamp and she tried to read herself to sleep. But, she just didn't know. She stirred, and there were stirrings inside her that she couldn't quite define, like the ripples on the pond when Mike skimmed a stone.

I'll scout for him at the Invitational, she told herself. Then, she turned off the lamp, hugged her pillow, and fell asleep.

"Hey Dad, what do you think of Amy?" Mike asked as he was hurrying out of the door on an errand, so he probably wasn't really expecting an answer. But, I tried, "Well Mike, I can't say that I know much about her." "What about Amy?" called Jan from the other room, but Mike was already on his way out, closing the door behind him. "What about Amy?" Jan repeated walking towards the front door and then watching out the front window as Mike drove away.

ELEVEN

Mike was wondering what to think about Amy, himself.

He thought about how he had embarrassed himself that first day at Crooked Branch. About how they had all laughed at him and his "mongrel" dog, even Amy, although she tried to conceal it, turning away with a blush to hide her dimpled smile. But, it was that blushing smile that gave her green eyes a glint of invitation and of inquisitiveness; so that he didn't really feel rejection when the others laughed at him, or Liam teased him. He wanted to answer her questions. He would stay, he and his funny, mongrel breed of a dog, and he would stay even if his dog failed to prove itself, he would show some other interest in their sport or in their dogs, or some other reason to come back to Crooked Branch, to come back and to continue to see her, to see her smile, to answer her questions, to ask some of his own.

And then, Rooster didn't let him down. Rooster made a go of it, and a show of it, and pointed a covey, and found the birds that Queenie didn't find, and he impressed them, Tom and Liam, and her, too. Rooster impressed her, even if he didn't, even if she thought him a dolt or whatever, his dog did him proud, and he could come again, and he would see her again, and would talk with her, and learn from her by asking her questions, and he would answer hers, if she asked them, like her eyes said that she would.

And, she did answer his questions, teaching him how to read dogs and to train dogs and to handle dogs and to ride horses. And she rode with him, not just following the dogs, but, then later that next summer, in the early evenings, when they rode together to the edge of the river that ran through Crooked Branch, where they didn't have to tend to any dogs, or to tend to Tom or Liam; but, could be free to let their minds to puzzle over their togetherness, at least his mind did, did hers? Did she find something in the rippling of the speckled water bubbling over river stones that looked rusty red and amber under the coralline clouds that, lazy river like, flowed before the sun as it lowered with a tint of ochre into the horizon? Did she find what he found there, there within the pulse of the rippling water and the spreading tincture of the sky? He couldn't bring himself to ask her; but, he wondered, and the wondering tugged at him; but, it couldn't tug the questions out of him. Not those questions. Not those questions that had nothing to do with the dogs or the horses; but, those other questions, the ones that asked what she thought or how she felt…that asked who she was. He couldn't ask those questions.

Then, suddenly she asked him such a question. He didn't expect it. Totally out of nowhere she asked him what he dreamt about. What kind of a question was that for a girl to ask a boy? And, how did he answer her? It was something dumb, he was sure. As he tries to recall it, it sounds even dumber still. Did he actually tell her that he dreamt about her? No, he couldn't have said that, how dumb would that have been? But, what did he say? He looked at her. He remembers looking into her eyes, briefly, after a moment, her green, inquisitive eyes.

Then she kissed him. Why did she kiss him? He must have said something that was really dumb for her to have wanted to kiss him. But, it wasn't really a kiss, not really. Just a peck, so maybe it wasn't all that dumb after all. She didn't act like it was dumb. She didn't look at him queerly, or walk away or anything. At least she didn't say, "That's cute, Mike." He could not have handled that, not "cute." They were grownups, after all, not kids. Kids can be cute, not grownups. Then the dogs barked and they panicked, and it was over, just like a dream is over when the alarm clock goes off.

So, what is he supposed to think about Amy? His dad is no help. He can't ask his mom for goodness sakes, she would think it was "cute." But, he can't stop thinking about her. She held his hand on the way home, and now she holds his thoughts. She holds them just as tenderly. He just doesn't know what to think about her. He'll see her later. He'll think about it then. He'll think about it tenderly.

TWELVE

Early Morning.

Our house, rear yard in the area of the flower garden, near the gray garden shed with its white shutters and its white door slightly ajar, an orange wheel barrow on its side against the outer wall, beneath the shed's only window, Rooster lying at the edge of the garden, sunning himself, Sparky milling about nearby. The blue butterfly arrives and lights on a yellow late-summer garden rose.

Butterfly:Hey guys. What's all the hubbub out front? What's with the RV?

Sparky:Hey. Where ya been? Family's getting ready for a trip to Virginia. That's why the RV. Put on a little weight, huh?

Butterfly:Been around. Yeah . . . those August blooms . . . hard to keep to my diet . . . especially the sneezeweed. I'll lose the weight flying south later this fall. What's in Virginia?

Sparky:Roo's gonna be in a championship. The whole family is going to watch him run, me too.

Butterfly:S'that right, Roo? A field trial championship? With quail? I've got some good friends among the Virginia quail. Virginia is a nice place this time of year. Still plenty of blooms...love that yellow loosestrife, um, um.

Rooster:(Rolling over and sitting up) Yup. Me n' Queen are in it. Mr. Quinn and Liam and Amy are going too.

Butterfly:Well, hey, mind if I come along? Folks won't mind, will they?

Rooster:Can't see that they would.

Sparky:Sure, you come along. Besides, we might need a friend among the quail. You never know, huh, Roo?

Later.

Me:Everybody in?

Jan:Yup.

Mike:All set.

Me:Okay, we're off and running.

Mike:Hey dad, did you see that? A blue butterfly just flew into the RV.

Jan:What? Where?

Me:Just leave a window open, Mike, it'll fly out again.

Jan:I don't see it.

Mike:Probably just flew back out again, strangest thing, though, that blue butterfly. Like when we first got Rooster.

The RV rolls down the road. It is early morning. The sky is clear and the sun is September bright. Sparky is standing on Jan's lap, looking out of the passenger window. Rooster curls up on the floor; the blue butterfly lies comfortably beneath his floppy, orange ear and begins to sing softly:

Get along little doggie
Get along little doggie
Over mountains and hills
Across rivers and streams
Get along little doggie
The trail we're riding
Is made of hopes and dreams

Rooster:Shhhhh.

THIRTEEN

It was the middle of the evening when we arrived at the site of the Invitational, the Jefferson Gorge Wildlife Refuge Area in the Shenandoah Valley of Virginia. We had a bit of trouble finding room for our RV among all of the other campers and the trailers with their strings of dogs and tethered horses alongside. Folks were busily milling about or sitting around small campfires finishing or just starting their dinners. We found a suitable spot, though, and after getting squared away, we set about to find Tom, Liam, and Amy, walking Rooster and Sparky on leash. We apparently were a sight to cause commotion, as voices picked up as we neared and got louder as we walked past. One scraggly looking fellow approached us with a glint of curiosity in his otherwise dark eyes, darker than the ever darkening evening sky.

"Well looky here, an orange dog to beat all get out. What do ya call that there dog? Hey come over here and take a look at this here orange dog," he called over his shoulder to a companion standing by a camper door, a beverage can in his hand. "This must be old Tom Quinn's orange dog, the one we've read about." His companion started over. Sparky began to growl, a deep, internal, guttural growl. "I'm Charley," he extended a hand, "and this here is my partner, Buck," indicating a shadowy fellow with the turn of his head. "Is that there Tom Quinn's dog?"

Buck arrived and reached to shake my hand, a sardonic smile dressing his ashen face. Sparky began to bark a high-pitched bark and to pull hard against his leash. "Sassy little dog, ain't he," Buck said. Jan picked Sparky up and attempted to quiet him down, but even in her arms the Big Spark continued his inhospitable growl, making a real nuisance of himself and attracting attention from other camps. Some folks stood to look, but none approached. You could just hear the murmurings going from camp to camp like echoes.

I shook Buck's hand. "No, this isn't Tom's dog," I said. "Rooster is our dog. Tom Quinn is his trainer, Tom and my son Mike, here." I indicated Mike with a slight nod of my head and twist of my shoulder. "Mike is Roo's handler, too." Mike nodded.

"Good for you, boy," Buck said to Mike, offering a hand that Mike accepted. "I like to see kids get involved in our sport." He looked Mike square in the eyes. "You up to handling a dog in an Invitational, kid?" He teasingly jabbed Mike on the shoulder. "I suppose that if you've worked with Tom Quinn, you should very well be. Charlie and me, we go way back with Tom. We taught him all he knows, ain't we Charlie?" Charlie nodded with a smirk. "Yup, all he knows," he grinned, turning to look over his shoulder.

"I guess so," Mike replied, looking away from Buck and towards me, and then to Jan, who continued to fuss with Sparky. The situation was uncomfortable, all the more so because of the increasing darkness as the night settled in without stars or moon. Mike shifted from foot to foot.

"Well, hey," I said, "have you seen Tom around? We just got here and we want to connect with him." I made to look about the camps, then at Jan and Mike for confirmation.

"He's down the road a bit," Tall Charlie answered, "him and Liam and his niece. We were just over there with him ourselves because we learned that we'll be braced with his dog tomorrow, first thing. Nice little setter he's got there. Queen, he said it was. Can't say we ever figured him for a setter guy. We're running our pointer, Red Eyes. You hear of Red Eyes? Might be you'll come up 'gainst him, should you qualify for the finals. We plan to be there, don't we, Buck?" Again, he looked over his shoulder, and then he turned to Buck.

Buck glanced coolly at Charlie, and then he stared probingly at Mike. "We first have to beat Tom's setter, Charlie." He drawled under leaden eyes, which he turned towards me.

"Well, hey, nice meeting you guys," I said, hoping my insincerity didn't show, and we began to take our leave. "We want to meet up with Tom before it gets too late. You say they put out the running order?" I asked and Charlie nodded. Buck again stared at Mike. "Well, come on Mike," I said. "Let's go find Tom and see if he knows when Rooster's running."

We turned to go. Mike hesitantly raised a hand in farewell. Jan put Sparky down and commanded him to heel. Sparky would repeatedly turn around and snarl until we finally lost sight of Tall Charlie and Buck in the darkness. Mike, too, looked back over his shoulder a few times. He was glancing over his shoulder when we came upon Tom's camp, Amy catching sight of us and calling us in.

After greetings, we told Tom how we had met Tall Charlie and Buck Arness along the dark road.

"They were just here," Tom said. "We're braced with them in the first race tomorrow. Liam isn't too happy about it." He turned to Liam, who shook his head slowly. "But, me, I'm looking forward to it." He clapped and rubbed his hands, turning to each of us with an Irish smile of glimmer and glitter.

"I don't like them," Mike said, looking from Liam to Tom and then to Amy.

"Queen beats their Red Eyes and we won't have to worry about them, Mike," Amy answered softly, looking down and stirring the ground with her foot. A crow took cawing flight from a nearby pin oak. Amy turned to pet Rooster.

We learned that Rooster wouldn't be running until Friday, in the third brace, paired with a pointer by the name of Sharp's Forester. How Queen might do we would not know until the morning came. We took our leave so that we could all get early to bed. As I would not do well telling about a dog's run in a field trial, this being just my very first, I will let Queen tell you about her race with Red Eyes, the way she told it to Rooster and Sparky.

FOURTEEN

"I knew that this would be an important race just from the fact that Tom would be my handler. Then, when Liam collared me to the line as a morning mist was slowly rising off the fields and beginning to shroud the tree lines, and I saw the size of the gallery…bigger than I had ever seen before…I really felt that this would be the most important race of my life. I was very proud, and very, very excited.

"But, I wasn't nervous, even though the night before I had overheard Tom and Liam talking about that Red Eyes dog and his handler. Even when I got near the line and I could see him, and I could scent the rancorous odor of his scout, that tall man, like some old, dried, wetland cabbage musk, I was too proud to be nervous. Even when that Red Eyes sneered at me and the spittle on his hair lipped fang glistened in the dank of the morning mist, I didn't get nervous. I just stood proud, firm, my forequarters dauntlessly forward, powerfully staunch. Jaw jutted forward, I regally declared, 'I am Queen.' He made no retort.

"Then, we were released, "*hie on*." He was very fast and powerful. I might have overtaken him, but I wanted to see his style. I wanted to see how he would work a bird. I wouldn't say that I trailed him exactly. I just didn't hunt on my own or try to overtake him. He made the first point not long into the race, just after the acres of sorghum in the open flat of browning blue stem and wild rye grasses. I honored, and everything was in order.

"We were released, and now I meant to take the front. I got the lead. There is a part of the course, a bend in the trail that takes you up over a knoll and beyond a stand of timber screened from the sight of the handlers and the gallery, and there I made my point, strong and hard on scent; I must have been ten yards from the good-sized covey. I was taut like a drawn bow. There was no breeze. The morning mist hovered horse head high. I knew it would be a while before Tom or Liam arrived. Then he did it! I couldn't believe it! I still to this moment can't believe it.

"Red Eyes came right in and stole my point, got right in front of me by several yards, putting me at a second honor. I heard yodeling not far off, and I knew that I dared not try to retake my point lest I be the one thought stealing. I stood my ground. My temper boiled, and my panted breath was like tea kettle steam as it rose to meet the ceiling of the morning mist. I heard the cawing of crows in the woods, then the screech of a hawk.

"I looked back as Tom approached. I could see disappointment on his face. Then the quail covey was flushed, and it flew squawking in all directions, and the shot was made, and there was a murmured approval from the gallery, and then Tom just commanded me to continue, and the tone of his voice was like I'd not heard from him before, and I just became angrily determined, vengeful, and I ran fast and hard, but I could not get to the front of that thieving Red Eyes. He is a strong dog...a vigorously fast dog. I could not catch him.

"I couldn't. There was no way I was gonna put myself in another honor situation, but I couldn't catch him and I couldn't get off course, not as it spread into this large pasture of tall, yellow green grasses and flowering Virginia forbs. There were no birds there, though. Not even among the Joe Pye or other weeds, or around the red cedar, where you might expect them. Again I heard a hawk scream and I saw it circle above the forest. Where there is a hawk there are quail. I saw Red Eyes go in. I followed him. I heard Tom call after me, 'Aye yup, Queen, come around,' loud and harsh like he meant it. I ignored him. I was pursuing a thief and was set on him.

"The still mist was thick in the woods, and there was no path to follow. This was rocky ground and the terrain sloped steeply upward. There were tall black walnuts and pignut hickories, black cherries and various oaks forming a thick upper story of leafy green ochre and sheen. There was an understory of chinquapin, sweet bay and paw paw, all in verdant of myrtle, moss and brown. And, there were big tooth aspen and hornbeam with their pale green leaves, so I was certain we would find grouse among the shrubwood, even if there were no quail. The fragrance of the spicebush was strong upon the forest mist, but not so strong as to cover bird scent. Even if I could not see Red Eyes, I would know where he would be going.

"I ran hard up the rocky grade, slipping at times on loose stones. I found Red Eyes standing at the top where the mist hung thick as fog. I heard distant yodels from the handlers behind us, and the sound of the scouts' horses cracking upon the slope stones and the sticks and pine needles of the forest floor. I knew that I could not be seen. I rushed forward to wrest the point from that thief in a red mask.

"In my rage and haste, I didn't notice that Red Eyes was not on point at all. He had merely stopped at the ridge above the steep drop into the Jefferson Gorge. I ran past him. He should have warned me, but he didn't. I stumbled on loose stone, then fell hard and tumbled down. It was all so blurry in the mist. I rolled, and then slid on my belly. I was clawing the ground in an effort stop or slow my plunge. I could see him watch my fall, sneering, spittle glistening on his fang. I felt fear and panic and anger.

"The next thing that I remember, I heard Mike and Amy calling. I lay near the bottom of the ravine, against the trunk of a buckeye that stopped my fall. I picked myself up. I tried to climb out. My right foreleg would not hold my weight and I fell again, slipping a bit along the downhill pitch. I yelped. They heard me. Mike struggled slowly down the slope to rescue me. I heard him announce his approach. 'I'm coming Queen,' he said, 'I'm coming girl.' He carried me up the slope, stumbling at times as his feet would lose their hold on the broken slate. He cradled me to Amy, and I rode back laying across Amy's saddle.

Now, here I am…my leg in a cast. I'm sad for Tom. I was a vengeful fool, but that Red Eyes is the devil's dog."

FIFTEEN

We in the gallery could only watch when Queen and Red Eyes entered the woods. The scouts, Liam and Tall Charlie, hurried to follow. There being no clear trail for their horses, the scouts' progress was slowed by the undergrowth and low tree limbs. They never reached the crest of the gorge.

After Queen's fall, Red Eyes resumed his hunt lower down the slope. Tall Charlie found him near the forest edge, on point beneath an aspen, where he marked a native grouse among some spicebush with bright red berries. Charlie called out for the handler, and Buck and Judge Darrell York followed the call. Liam continued to search for Queen as Buck made his flush. When Red Eyes was released, Liam returned to Tom in the pasture.

"Did Queen come back out?" Liam asked.

Tom shook his head. "Nope, I imagine she is continuing on a run to the front, perhaps still in the woods." He gave a holler, "Come around, Queen." Then he instructed Liam to remain just inside the wood line, as he himself, would continue along the pasture course, within sight of the judges as the rules required. "If she wasn't backing that other dog's point on that grouse, then she probably had scent of her own that she's following. You'll either find her on point further up, or she'll come back out. She knows how to run a course." He gave another holler, "Aye up, Queen, come around."

Red Eyes returned to the pasture course. He ranged well to the front, hunting hard and fast. The course extended far to the horizon, dotted here and there with singular cedars and interrupted only by copses of alder, birch and oak, their leaves a burnished green in late September, all hemmed in on the east by the woods where Liam conducted his search, but there continued to be no sign of Queen.

Although the yellowing bluestem pasture grasses were tall, they did not conceal the big pointer, and he was observable even at a far distance. Once again he was seen on point, and the party moved apace to cover the ground to the flush. But still there was no sign of Queen. When the flush was completed all in order, Judge York turned to Tom.

"Twenty minutes," he said, and that was all that needed saying.

Tom turned his horse away. Without speaking to anyone, he rode towards the wood line and shouted loudly, "Twenty minutes, Liam." He repeated, "Twenty minutes…Liam." There was a weakness in his voice. I turned to Mike for an explanation.

"If a dog is out of judgment for twenty minutes, Dad, then it's disqualified." He turned towards Amy. Her eyes were tearing. "Should we go, too?" He asked her. She nodded slowly. "Dad, Amy and I are going to help find Queen. You just follow along with the gallery, and we'll meet you back at the RV." They pulled off and headed towards Tom.

Liam came out from the woods. "No sign of her," he told Tom.

"I've got to believe that she's running to the front," replied Tom. That's the way she's been trained. These woods go on for a long time. They follow the gorge. Let's keep riding forward, but I've got to stay down off that rocky slope, my hip is bothering me enough already. You take the upper course, Liam." He shook his head despondently.

"Tom…Mike and I will back track." Amy said. "I know Queen would always run to the front, but maybe she got turned in the dense undergrowth or in that mist. That could explain why she didn't come around for your call. She wouldn't run off. We will find her and catch up with you, or we'll meet you back at camp." She turned her horse and Mike followed. I saw concern in his eyes, and felt the need to accompany him, but I left it to him and Amy. They're not kids, after all, and somehow, in a saddle, in a field that's damp with morning mist and edged by trees in early autumn, you look upon your son differently when he's called upon to fulfill some responsibility, and you let him go.

I continued in the gallery.

SIXTEEN

Later, at camp, Liam paced about, ruing the race with Red Eyes. "I feared that no good would come from running with a red marked dog belonging to Buck Arness," he said. "There is badness in that man and in that Tall Charlie, too. I've always believed that they sabotaged your saddle that time when you broke your hip, Tom." He stopped pacing and picked up some sheet of paper from the camp table. He crumbled the paper in his hands and then threw it in the fire. "Whatever evil is in them is in their dog, too. I blame that Red Eyes for Queen's fall, just as if he pushed her off that ledge."

Tom was in a good deal of discomfort. The long time in the saddle had aggravated his arthritis and caused his hip to pain. "No sense regretting what's done, Liam," he said with a grimace. We didn't pick the brace mate. I wasn't going to not run Queen just on account of Buck Arness or Charlie Hinkle, dang them. Queen earned the right to be here. I don't attribute any malice to a brut animal. The way that pointer was running, Queen wasn't likely to qualify anyway. There would've been too many honors. I'm just sorry she's injured." He reached down and scruffed behind Queen's ear as she lay asleep by his feet.

Our despair in Queen's misfortune weighed on us throughout the night. The next day, though, we found reason for optimism after Rooster's performance in his brace with Sharp's Forester. Tom had been unable to gallery because of his soreness, so Liam related to him what had happened.

"Well...I'll tell you...that Rooster...he's got field trial in him, alright. As if we didn't know that already. But, each time he runs, you see it again, and you say, 'what's that funny looking, orange dog doing out there?' and then he just shows you. I'll tell you, it was something to watch, and the gallery was taken with him too, at least at the end," Liam began.

"Well, what'd he do, Liam, gosh darn it." Tom was impatient in his discomfort.

"Okay," Liam continued. "Well...he had six solid, all in order finds, more than any other dog in the competition so far, and two good honors to boot. Plus, he finished strong. Mike handled him real well...kept him well to the front with quick flushes, not wasting any time. There was a lot of buzz when he was done, I'll tell you that. I'd say he's got as good a chance as any dog here to make it to the finals on Sunday."

"You really think so?" I asked with pleasant surprise. Mike and Amy both nodded their heads in agreement. "He ran real well, Dad," Mike added, looking to Amy for confirmation, then to Jan to see what impression the news was making. She showed a mother's pride and affection for both boy and dog.

"We'll know tonight…when they announce the braces," Tom responded to Liam with a twitch of pain as he shifted his weight in his chair.

When evening came, the news was both exciting and troubling. Rooster was among only six finalists. But he would be braced with Red Eyes in the last race of the day. This was surely an unfortunate development, and Liam protested vehemently as we gathered in our RV. "Those folks are no good and their Red Eyes is no good, and I don't want another one of our dogs running with him or them."

Strangely, however, Tom seemed to welcome the news, the look on his face suggesting some new-found strength and determination despite his ailments. "If we send them back to Missouri with a loss to a mongrel dog, Liam, old Duke Arness, bless his soul, will roll over in his grave and spite his boy for running a red marked dog. We can do it, Liam. Rooster can do it. I saw a rainbow with an orange arc in a dream before we left. That orange, mongrel dog with the floppy ears and yellow eyes will be their comeuppance sure enough… and Deputy's redemption." His eyes had a far-away look with the moist glisten of a smile's tear.

Liam shook his head, "we don't need another dog hurt."

At that moment, Sparky began to scratch at the RV door to go out. Jan got his leash and opened the door to take him for a walk when she exclaimed, "Hey, did you see that? A blue butterfly just flew out of the RV. Must be the same one that Mike saw when we left home, oddest thing, huh? Imagine that it stayed in the RV all of this time. And it was blue. I don't believe that I have ever seen a blue butterfly before." But, no one else had seen the butterfly, except for Sparky and Rooster.

"Where the heck is she going?" A curious Sparky looked up at Rooster.

"I don't know," Rooster answered uncertainly. "She said something about going to speak with some quail."

Down the road, in the dark, by a small campfire, Buck's pointer laid ambuscade, the fire's glow devilishly reflected in the blacks of his red masked eyes.

Buck stirred the fire with a stick.

SEVENTEEN

The day broke in a heavy drizzle, but it was forecast to clear. Nearby, a yellow-bellied woodpecker drummed upon a black cherry tree.

We met at Tom's camper to make preparations for the race. Amy insisted on brushing Rooster. "It's relaxing," she said as she took the brush along down his bearded muzzle. Mike and Liam fed and saddled four horses, although only Liam intended to gallery the first two braces.

Jan was too nervous to gallery Rooster's race, and Tom was still unable to ride. I moved the RV to a hilltop with a good view of the course. There they could sit on the rooftop and watch what might be seen with the aid of Tom's binoculars. I carried camp chairs up top for them, and a small cooler with water, pop and chips, and they settled in as sporting spectators are wont to do at similar events.

Jan was holding Sparky on her lap, when suddenly the blue butterfly lit before them on the edge of the roof. "Do you see it, Tom," she whispered, "Do you see the blue butterfly?"

"I do see it," he answered softly, "a blue butterfly, surely enough it's a pooka. I've not seen one since I was a child in Ireland."

"Did you know, Janice," he continued with a timber of reminiscence in his voice, "that long ago, Ireland had great forests of spruce, fir, and yew. There was blackthorn and oak, hawthorn, alder and downy birch, all with an understory of buckthorn and goat willow, and shrubs of silver queen with bright red berries in the winter, and red cascade with orange berries in autumn…forests not unlike those that rim this here course. In these forests dwelt leprechauns and woodland sprites or pookas that were animal spirits incarnate.

"Then, the forests were hewed and timbered for the ships of England's navy …there are no more forests in Ireland today, you know…and the leprechauns and sprites had nowhere to live. The leprechauns simply made themselves invisible. They still live among the Irish today, once in a while actually delivering a promised pot of gold as ransom to the child that catches one while dreaming. But the sprites did not have the power of invisibility, or any pots of gold to pay their ransom. In order to conceal themselves from those who might capture and cage them, the sprites changed their form, becoming blue butterflies."

He addressed the butterfly. "So, what are you doing here, little pooka?" The blue butterfly fluttered up and lit on his knee. "Oh, here to watch the race, are you? You must be from County Galway. Well then, let's watch the race together." He said. Sparky turned to look at Tom and the blue butterfly, and then he rested his head on Janice's arm.

Liam returned before the end of the second brace. "It's time to get ready," he said without dismounting.

"How did those other braces go, Liam?" Tom asked.

"Not well," Liam replied, shaking drizzle from his hat. "The first brace only found three birds, one a native grouse among some laurel along the forest edge. It was a difficult flush. I think that the second brace might have gone birdless…well one of the dogs, Wild Bill Crossley's pointer was picked up early because it had a nonproductive, and Canada Sam's dog produced no game, although it covered the sorghum and pasture well enough. I had to leave early to get back here and get ready, so maybe it found something towards the end, along the bottom land. There are good clumps of berry weeds and red cedar down in that hollow.

"I don't understand it, though. They put out plenty of quail before the first brace and more for the second. There should have been plenty of birds out there. Those were good dogs, or else they wouldn't be in the finals. Maybe it was the early drizzle. Wet birds can be a problem. Now that the rain is stopping and the sun's starting to come out, we should be able to do better than the two birds found by Big Lou's setter in the first brace. We'll see. Sometimes it's just the luck of the day. Well, let's go. You ready, Mike?"

"I'm ready," Mike answered and he turned to Amy, "Amy?"

Amy had already started to leash Rooster, which was answer enough. Mike got his horse, as did I, for there was no way I would stay a spectator atop the RV, and we walked together towards the line. There the gallery was astride, impatiently waiting…the judges, too, though they were busy writing their notes of the last brace. As we reached the line, I put a hand on Mike's shoulder.

"This will be good," I told him. "No matter how it goes, you can be darn proud of yourself and your dog. Your mom and I are proud, too. Give it a good effort." Then we both turned to watch as Amy collared Rooster to the line, Liam riding along side, leading her horse.

They were intercepted by Buck. "Sending kids to do men's work, Liam?" he sneered, "Where's Tom?" Then he spit tobacco juice over the opposite side of his gelding.

Liam stopped to answer Buck, while Amy continued on. He looked from Buck to Tall Charlie and Red Eyes, who were already at the line, and then back to Buck. "Tom's not well enough to ride," he said, and then he added reprovingly, "We're sending a dog to win a trophy. The kids only have a small part, which I suspect that they'll do well enough. You needn't be concerned for none but yourself and your dog."

Then he straightened himself in his saddle, establishing his full size and his strength from years working a farm. He leaned towards Buck and was firm. "I don't much care for you, Arness," he said. "Anything goes wrong out there, anything at all, and I will come looking for you and Charlie. This won't be like the time Tom was thrown from his saddle." His eyes had a steely glint.

Buck disdainfully tipped his cap, turned aside and rode away.

EIGHTEEN

Although the rain had stopped, the morning was still overcast with drifting clouds.

I took a place among the assembled gallery. Mike was to the fore, atop Tom's gray gelding, wearing oil tin chaps over his Wrangler jeans, a faded yellow barn jacket and an old, tan Boston Red Sox baseball cap over his bit-too-long-for-my-liking brown hair. Amy, her auburn hair in a ponytail drawn through the back strap of her navy blue cap, also in denim jeans, but with a hooded, green windbreaker, brought Rooster to the line. Red Eyes paid them no mind. Tall Charlie leered at them and then turned back to Buck with a scoff. Buck shrugged dismissively.

I was joined by Liam. One man in the gallery, a fellow in a green cap with a tractor insignia, mentioned to Liam that no quail had been found during the second brace. Liam began to express his surprise, when Judge Ros Trigg inquired of the handlers' readiness. Just that quickly the dogs were released, "*hie on.*"

Red Eyes flashed to the front and as hard and strong as Rooster might run, it was clear that he would be no match for the pointer. Just as the dogs entered the near sorghum fields, Mike caracoled left towards the westerly tree line in the hopes of pulling Rooster off the pointer's trail. He gave a yodel, but Rooster would not veer. The first bird found belonged to Red Eyes, Rooster placed in honor. Atop the RV, Tom passed the binoculars to Janice without words.

The man in the green cap remarked for any who might hear, "That mongrel dog is no match for that big pointer."

Sure enough, when the dogs were released off that first point, Red Eyes quickly put distance between himself and Rooster. Again Mike attempted to call Rooster off the trail, "Roo, aye up…around," but Rooster stayed his course, a little to Mike's frustration, Amy's too.

"That orange dog will just tail that pointer the whole race, might as well just pick 'im up right now," jeered the man in the green hat. Liam moved away from him. I followed.

At about 20, the second bird was found in the pasture by Red Eyes. For all that might otherwise be said of this dog, or of his handlers, I have to concede that he was impressive on point, his coat tightly stretched across a pulsing chest of well-defined ribs, his tail ram rod straight. Unhesitant, unflinching, his whole visage was one of defiant power. He looked a shootist at his trade, his red mask defining him as an outlaw. I despaired for Rooster, who again was compelled to honor. I looked to Liam, who just shook his head slowly and said nothing.

At the RV, Tom huffed in exasperation. Sparky left Jan's lap and walked to the roof's edge, as if to obtain a better view. The butterfly joined him.

"That's going to be the C Team," the butterfly said. "There are three of them. They've laid a strong covey scent and then they separately snuck away to bury deep in the grasses. They'll be difficult to rise to the flush." You would swear that a butterfly could grin, if it had teeth.

Sure enough, Buck was having a hard time making flush. Repeatedly he looked back towards his pointer, advanced several steps and swept new ground with his kicks. Nothing rose. Judge York reminded him that his time was running out. "There's a bird here," Buck retorted, "or else my dog wouldn't be standing." "It is the finals," York allowed. "So, I will let you have a bit more time, but I'm sending the other dog on." With that he turned to Mike and told him that he could pull Rooster off the honor and continue.

Tom looked to Janice a bit bemused and handed her the binoculars. "It appears they're allowing Arness additional time to produce a bird," he told her. "The judges don't want to disqualify a dog in the finals without a fair chance, especially if the dog appears to be in the running for a ribbon. They're freeing Rooster off his back, though. That could be good news. Now he may get to the front, and he should be able to mark his own finds. If he's going to have any chance in this competition at all, he needs to work birds, not just honor his brace mate. It was difficult for Queen against that masked dog. I don't know about Rooster, but it's not over yet. He's got the strength. He just needs to find some birds to work."

The butterfly turned to Sparky, "Wait until you see the B team, Spark."

NINETEEN

Breezes brushed away the remnants of the morning's clouds, clearing the day and carrying along game scent from distant haunts.

Rooster broke hard when released from his honor. Mike, Amy and Judge York followed. We of the gallery remained arrears of Red Eyes' point so as not to interfere by sound or commotion as Buck attempted to make flush.

Bird scent pulled Rooster out of the fields and towards the westerly woods bordering the gorge. He weaved through the tree line. Mike tried to call him down, "Roo…come around…ahead…aye up." Amy looked over her shoulder to assess the progress of the brace mate. She said nothing.

In a very short time, Buck flushed a single quail and made shot. Roo looked back to the crack of the gun, but he did not slow his dash. Red Eyes was released and broke hard and fast to regain the course. He, too, soon left the grasses to take to the woodland edge, drawn by the same wind carried scents and bent on overtaking his rival.

Rooster went into the woods. Red Eyes followed, rapidly closing their gap. A group of yellow warblers burst from the treetops with whistled alarm. A crow cawed.

Within the woodland shadows, Rooster locked up on point, just slightly up the slope leading to the ridge above the gorge. There, quail were hid in a thicket of faded green chinquapin surrounding two yellowing aspens.

Red Eyes quickly came upon Rooster. He slowed to a prowl, almost like a big cat, like a tiger, and then he began to steal forward, probing Rooster's guard. Rooster noted his presence, but did not flinch from his mark. Seeing and hearing no challenge, Red Eyes stole the point.

Rooster was unsure how to respond to such unabashed thievery. Never before had a brace mate usurped his point. He thought a moment…thought of Queen…then slowly extended one leg forward in a cautious attempt to reestablish his primacy.

Red Eyes fiercely growled, "Try it, yeller eyes, and I'll rip yer floppy ears right off of your head. You mongrels ain't got no business in this sport of mine. I'll tell ya now, no dang mongrel mutt is gonna deny me no prize, that is for sure. They should've culled you as a pup. Stand and be content with your honor, mutt." There was fire in his eyes that glowed all the brighter in the darkness of the forest shadows.

I told you earlier that the cowboy conceit does not apply to a dog like Rooster; it is not a gun slinger by nature or nurture. Rooster could not answer this hostility with a slap of leather, a quick draw and a dead eye. He stood frozen and uncertain. He timidly withdrew the leg that he had put forward. He stood. He thought again of Queen. Something stirring within him swelled into defiance.

Boldly he began to step forward, determined to fearlessly challenge the thief's threat with all of his strength and will. Then he suddenly heard the approach of the scouts' horses, the crush of leaves, twigs and stones beneath their steel shod hooves. He heard Amy's yodel.

Forlorn, he stopped, and he stood still in honor of Red Eyes' point, dispirited. Chest fallen, with a burning in his heart, its wings on fire, he stood. He dared not be caught creeping and himself be thought a thief. He fought not to let his anger or dismay show knowing that he remained under judgment, and that his honor must be as staunch as his point.

He saw Tall Charlie approach and heard him yell down the slope, "Dog's on point." He heard Amy yell, "Dog's standing." He heard commotion as Mike, Buck, and the judges entered the woods. He stood his mark as they arrived. He stood in proper honor of Red Eyes, not needing Mike's cautionary, "Easy, Rooster." He even feigned pride.

He stood as Buck dismounted and moved to flush the quail from out of the yellowing chinquapin. He stood as several quail frantically made flight and Buck made shot. And…he stood in surprise and disbelief, as did all in witness, as one of the quail soared straight up and then, like a hawk attacking prey, swiftly and directly swooped straight back down again, pecked Red Eyes on the top of his head, and then flew off over the ridge and across the gorge.

Unlike Tom's fabled dog of years gone by, Red Eyes did not stand his point upon the quail's attack. He broke. He gave a growling and furious chase, and he was disqualified.

Buck threw his hat on the ground, kicked it, cursed, picked up the hat, cursed some more; then he mounted his horse, glared at Liam and he and Tall Charlie rode off to recover their frothing and wayward dog last seen a howling into the gorge. Mike and the two judges renewed the stake, Rooster hie on without a brace mate.

But, Rooster had not yet scored a point, and time was running short. If he was going to earn a placement at the Invitational, then he needed to work some birds of his own, and quickly. "Find a bird!" Mike encouraged him with urgency. "Go!"

TWENTY

"Rooster has come out of the woods," Tom told Jan as he watched through his binoculars. "Mike's come out, too…and the judges are with him… both of them. That's odd. There's Amy. I see her. But I don't see Buck's dog… or him…or Charlie. Something's up." He glassed the field and then handed the binoculars to Jan. "If both judges are with Mike, then Buck's dog is out of judgment. The dog must have been picked up or it might have run off. Well I'll be a son of a gun."

"That would've been the B Team," the Butterfly reported to Sparky. I do assure you that butterflies can grin, even if they have no teeth to show. Sparky's grin, on the other hand, is very toothy. Sparky grinned.

"Does that mean that Rooster wins?" Jan asked excitedly, lowering the binoculars and rocking nervously on her seat.

"No, no," answered Tom. "There are still the other dogs that have run. And Rooster hasn't had a point or worked a bird of his own, yet…unless he did so in the woods. All that honoring of Buck's dog won't get him a placement. If he doesn't work birds off his own point, then he's done for. What time is it?" Looking at his watch, he answered his own question. "There isn't much time left."

"Wait until you see the A Team," the Butterfly giddily whispered to the Havanese.

When Rooster came out of the woods, he almost immediately was drawn across to the far side of the pasture, where it was separated by a slender tree line from an adjacent field of sweet sorghum, fallow in the early fall. He crossed the tree line, a course not taken in earlier competitions, and there, just on the other side, he came hard on point.

"There isn't time to be going off course," Amy warned Mike. They hurried their gait so as to quickly reach Rooster's mark. The judges showed no favor with their own pace, and we in the gallery were marshaled at a walk. I felt nervous pangs of impatience and feared disappointment. Liam glanced at his watch.

Michael reached Roo's point and quickly dismounted. Handing the reins to Amy, he hurriedly took long strides to make the flush. A native grouse lifted. Mike made shot and released the dog. Rooster broke like captured lightning freed from an uncorked bottle. He stayed awhile scouring in the sorghum, and then he crossed the tree line back into the pasture.

"There are no birds in this pasture," Liam worried, slowly shaking his head and looking again at his watch. "He's got to get down into the bottom fields, among some alder or red cedar where the birds might be coveyed. His time is running out. That last point was at around 80…there isn't but ten minutes left."

Rooster was not running a line. He hunted in a pattern, like a backwards Z. His run would not take him straightaway to the bottom field, as Liam had wanted, nor did Mike think to direct him there as he might have done with a call to "get ahead." If Liam was correct that there would not be any birds until the lower acres of switch grass and cedar groves, then time might expire before Rooster had another point.

Judge York drew back his shirt sleeve and looked at his wristwatch. He turned towards Judge Trigg.

The man in the green cap announced to no one in particular, "That mongrel dog's all done."

I glanced over at Liam, who had a haggard look, like that of a dust covered cowboy after a long day in the saddle.

Back atop the trailer, Tom whispered, mostly to his self, "Come on, dog. Come on, Rooster." Then louder, "Come on, dang it, Roo. By the shamrocks of the Old Sod, come on you darn mongrel dog."

Janice stood up from her camp chair and grasped Tom's shoulder tightly with her left hand.

And then…

Well, you may take this for the truth, as this is how it was reported in the October 13, 2009 edition of *The National Field*:

"…The Quinn dog came off his sorghum field point hell bent for leather, as if he understood that his time was short. He covered the upper pasture of greenish yellow grasses, but was birdless. He crossed the slope of the breezy knoll overlooking the lower field and ran strong to mid-field. Just as we ourselves crested the knoll, he suddenly slammed hard on point, his course-haired, orange coat pulled so tight about his throbbing flesh that his ribs appeared near to breaking through. The young handler looked to the judges for approval, and then he urged his horse into a lope to reach the dog's mark under the gun. His scout followed. We then saw what we all agree we had never seen before in the sport of field trials, or in any other adventure of man and beast in woods and fields.

Upon arrival at his dog, the handler quickly dismounted, dropped the horse's reins, looked to his dog, and perhaps even said a word or two that we could not hear at our distance. Then he put a dozen or more quail to flight with the single, broad sweep of his boot. But the birds did not merely fly off and away in a squawking frenzy, not even at the crack of the handler's shot. They flew up and then circled overhead in aeronautic acrobatics of eddying loops and swoosh dips and spiraling curls and tumbles, all above and about the youth and his dog, their circle expanding in a fluttering synchronized flight seemingly in homage and acclaim. They only dispersed in diverse directions as the gallery neared. All but one, this last bird swooped down upon the orange dog as if to attack, but then waived its wings in full glide, pulled up and away, and flew off to join its covey mates, the orange dog never flinching from his point.

Then it was all over. There was no need to wait for the judges' decision. We had all seen the winner acknowledged by his quarry."

Amy dismounted and joined Mike. She held his hand and together they watched the last bird fly away. Then she turned to him and they hugged and kissed a tender but hurried kiss, not wanting to be embarrassed before our gallery. She rested her head briefly on his shoulder. The late afternoon September sun nestled softly on cumulus clouds lazing still high above the horizon.

TWENTY ONE

Mike, who has been there, tells me that at the thoroughbred race track in County Galway, in the Old Sod, horses race backwards. I have a hard time imagining horses running backwards. Michael is a truthful fellow, but he is something of a poet, and poets invent things.

For example, Mike has told me about a creature of the American West that is like a jack rabbit, but with antlers. A jackalope, it's called. I have been to the West, and I have never seen such a creature. Mike says that's because jackalopes are too fast to be seen. I think that Mike invented the jackalope, but I'm not sure. I know that he once wrote a poem about it.

Poets are storytellers. Mike is the source for much of this story about Rooster. He supplied all of the dialogue between the animals, which he assures me was accurately transcribed from what he had overheard or what was reported to him by Sparky. Well, he or Amy, he says, but I think that Amy is a co-conspirator of the invention.

Of course, Tom Quinn had poetry in him, too. So, I think that perhaps he also conspired with Michael in the telling of this story about Rooster. I'm quite sure, for example, that Michael did not know about pookas or of the origin of the blue butterfly until he learned about them from Tom. And, I further suspect that Tom pretty much invented the quail conspiracy.

Nonetheless, although I have never seen a horse race backwards or a jackalope in Wyoming, I did see what I saw that day at the Jefferson Gorge Wildlife Refuge, when a floppy-eared, orange, mongrel-breed of a dog named Rooster did, indeed, win the National Field Trial Invitational, and you need not just take my word for it, because Sparky saw it too, and you can ask him.

Sparky will tell you, too, that there were other adventures later on, although perhaps none so memorable. It's just that I didn't go along, leaving it to the kids. The kids and old Tom, as they were best suited for the dreams and imaginings of which such adventures are often made.

The pooka? Oh, she's probably flitting about here somewhere. Look around. If you see her, make a sound like a tree, whisper like an aspen leaf in a gentle breeze, and she may come to you, and may sniff your hand.

It's like Amy told Mike that summer at the barn, remember? If you can imagine, then you can believe, and then it will be true that there are pookas and faeries, and leprechauns and pots of gold at the end of the rainbow. And, if you believe, then you soon may find:

A shamrock or a wish bone
A fern seed or a shooting star
A rabbit's foot or a horseshoe
Along the trails that you carve
Over mountains and hills
Across rivers and streams
The trails we're riding
Are made of hopes and dreams

Did you enjoy the chocolate milk?

AUTHOR AND ROOSTER

Painting by Rosalind Trigg, Trigg Studio,
Lexington, Kentucky

Edward Pontacoloni resides in Lake George, New York with his wife, Janice. His children, Eddie, Nicholas, Denise and Michael are grown.

Rooster was born on February 5, 2001 and christened Ruff Creek Jebadiah. Jebadiah is a biblical name associated with both companionship and woodsmanship.

Rooster never was a field trial dog of any merit. He did win a CASDA walking, All Age Championship one year, and he received a fourth place ribbon in a Brittany Amateur Open Dog horseback stake another year. His best race was probably run in a later Gordon Setter Amateur Open Dog horseback stake, although he wasn't awarded a placement. It was a memorable race, though, at least so said the gallery. "Made history," they said. Although a "mongrel breed," Rooster is registered in the Field Dog Stud Book of the American Field Sporting Dog Association.

Rooster was a very dear friend and hunting companion. He went to rest on September 16, 2014 and is buried in Lake George, New York.